Kitten

MINE

Kitten

KAY MAREE

Contents:

Kitten Mine

Cover Design © Designed With Grace -
http://www.designedwgrace.com/
Cover Images © Adobe Stock & Deposit Photos
Editing – Susan Horsnell & Word Writer Pro

Dedication

Thank you to my wonderful husband, and my three beautiful children. Everything I do is because of you. You make every day brighter.

To my parents and mother in-law, thank you for supporting me, and listening to me talk about my characters like they are real people.

To my sister's Shantelle and Charmaine, thank you for loving me through the highs and lows, and always being there to support me.

Tiffany, I could never thank you enough for being my sounding board throughout the writing of this book. If it wasn't for you, I probably wouldn't have finished this story. You were there to listen to me, support me, deal with my crazy, and I thank you mostly for just being you. I am blessed to have you in my life.

Social Links

Facebook:
https://www.facebook.com/kay.maree.334
Twitter:
https://twitter.com/MisKay85
Goodreads:
https://www.goodreads.com/book/show/34528910-
angel-mine?ac=1&from_search=true
Goodreads Author Page:
https://www.goodreads.com/user/show/65394903-kay-
maree

About the Author

I live in Newcastle, on the New South Wales coast of Australia with my husband and three beautiful children.

Between being a taxi for my children, and working full-time, I somehow find the time to write. It's something I love with a passion and with the encouragement of my very supportive husband, I have accomplished one of my dreams – releasing my first novel.

I hope you fall in love with my characters as much as I have.

I love reading and getting lost in a good book when I manage to snatch five minutes to myself.

Kay Maree

Prologue

After slamming my bedroom door shut, I dive on the bed, and bury my head in the pillows, hugging the teddy bear from my father close to my chest while trying to block out the screaming going on downstairs.

"Why would you think it's ok to take your little sister to that party?" Mom yells.

"Mom, nothing happened." My sister's words sound slightly slurred.

"That's not the point. You're older, you know better than this, and instead of looking after her you got drunk and left her to fend for herself."

"So, I'm not supposed to have fun because I have to

look out for her?"

"You're supposed to take some responsibility and look out for your sister"

Pushing my head deeper into my pillows so I can't hear them anymore, I wish I could take back telling mom where I was because I know my sister will turn this around on me. It's always the way. Suddenly, my door flies open. Ashley, my sister, is standing in the doorway with a pissed off look on her face.

"This is all *your* fault. If you had kept your mouth shut, none of this would have happened."

"I'm sorry, I didn't think mom would have been home from work."

"You're the reason everything has turned to shit. You're the reason daddy left and now mom says we have to move back to Newcastle. You're the reason I won't be able to see my boyfriend anymore. When are you going to stop being mommy's little girl and grow the fuck up?"

She rushes at me and I cower. She grabs me roughly, digging her nails into my arms. I cry out as I feel her nails break the skin

"My friends are right about you, you're pathetic and ugly. No wonder you have no friends."

"That's not true I have, Brooklyn." I defend myself in a weak voice.

"She won't be your friend when she finally wises up and sees how pathetic you really are."

I gaze through tear-filled eyes into the eyes of my sister, not recognizing who she is anymore. Ever since daddy left, she has been different. I use to look up to her and wanted to be just like her when I got older. With her beautiful blonde hair and tanned skin, size 8 figure. She's perfect. Me? I have fiery red hair, pale skin and curves.

Her words hurt every bit as much as the things she does to me. I feel like I owe her, not being the good sister she deserved. I'm not clever like Ashley either. I do okay in school, but I'm not the smartest person. I don't have a lot of friends. I have Brooklyn and when we don't have school we're constantly together. I'm not sure how I'll cope if we move away from here.

I run my finger over the recent cut on my wrist hidden under my watch, Ashley looks down and notices what I'm doing.

"Why don't you save us all the trouble and do it already, I'm sick of hearing you cry every night. You're broken and that will never change."

She pushes me back onto the bed and I watch through tear-filled eyes as she leaves my bedroom. I wait until I hear the door shut before I crawl under the covers, pull my diary out, and let the worthlessness I feel out.

Dear Diary,

Why did I open my mouth, why do I ruin everything I touch?

It's all my fault. If only I was a better sister, maybe then Ashley would like me.

No wonder daddy left. I'm so pathetic.

I vow from this moment on, the only person I will trust is Brooklyn until she realizes I'm not worth the trouble and she walks away too.

I will build a wall around myself, one brick at a time, and keep pushing forward.

I will try to be stronger than the blade I hold in my hand.

I hate myself.

True to my mother's word, we packed up and moved back to Newcastle. She said it was time for a fresh start for all of us and we could be near our grandmother. Ashley seemed to get worse after we left. She was hardly ever home, and if she did come home, she was high or drunk. I'd be walking around on eggshells trying not to upset her. I learned to build a wall around myself and tried not to let anything she did or said hurt me, I had become so closed off, I wouldn't let anyone in. I didn't trust anybody, especially guys. Men usually said things to get what they wanted and then they would up and leave just like my father had. I wasn't going to let that happen. I was sad when Ashley went out one day and never came back, she was still my big sister, but I was relieved too. I no longer had to stay awake at night, worried she'd hurt me while I slept. She always threatened, I may not wake up in the morning.

About a year after we moved, mom became ill and my time was spent looking after her. I'd make sure she got to her appointments and the treatments she needed. I tried to contact Ashley, but she was always too busy or just didn't give a shit. In the end, I was the one to pick up the pieces and make sure everything got sorted when mom passed away. My grandma moved in with me to help out, but it ended up being me helping her. I didn't mind, but it wasn't the same - I still felt alone.

It was a sad and lonely time and the only person I had left besides grandma, was Brooklyn. She made me realize at least one person gave a shit about me. She understood me, and accepted me, for who I was. She understood why I'm the way I am. I don't know what I would have done if I didn't have her.

Chapter One

2 Months Earlier...

Katherine

Dear Diary,

Well, where do I start? I may as well get straight to the point, today was an exceptionally hard day. But, I did it; I had to. I pushed him away. It hurt like crazy; I struggled to breathe, so I built my wall back up and hid behind it, like I always do. It was hard as hell to walk away, but I can't allow him into my life. If I did, he would truly see how screwed up I am, and eventually leave me, just like my dad did. I doubt I could handle the devastation losing him would cause, and I may end up taking that blade and finally going through with it – ending my sad, sorry life.

You should've seen the hurt in his eyes when I turned my back on him at the cafe today. It about broke me, I almost changed my mind about my decision to push him away. I ran and hid in the Kitchen until I heard the doorbell and knew he had left.

I really wanted to tell Brooklyn how I felt, but then I would have to reveal my Secret. She's so happy, I don't want to affect that. She's my best friend, and after everything she has been through, I couldn't bring myself to dump my problems on her. Brooklyn knows something is wrong in my life and I know she is there for me, that she wants to help. But, I don't think anyone can help me. How do I burden someone so close with my problems, when I can't find the strength to help myself? I would never do it, especially to someone I love so dearly.

My mind plays on a damn loop all the time. Taunting me with how things could have been different, how I could have been different but, I am who I am. Nothing will change who I am. I have to accept, I'm just not good enough. It's why I built a wall around myself a long time ago. I needed to protect myself so people wouldn't know how deep their words hurt.

Antonio sees through me. He knows I'm not the person I show everyone else, that there is more to me than a sharp tongue. My scars are deep, carried inside and I'm afraid the wall I have carefully built around myself, will never be whole again. Whether I admit it or not, the fact is, he stole some of those bricks from me and I will never get them back. I did the right thing pushing him away before he gets too close and

13

shatters the rest of my wall. I have to keep reminding myself, because if I think anything else, if I let him in, he could break me into a million pieces that I will never be able to put back together again.

Taking a deep breath, I read the words again. Words that ring so true. Tears stream down my face and I close my eyes as I try not to run over all the questions in my head. I can't stop them. Why can't I be good enough? Why do I feel so broken? Why can't I have my happily ever after?

When I open my eyes, I look down at my diary and notice my tear drops have smudged some of the words. I'm angry, pissed off with myself, picking the diary up, I throw it across the room where it hits the wall before crashing to the floor. I sit looking toward the bathroom and see the glint of the razor sitting on my sink, taunting me, knowing it won't be long before I will want to feel the sting of the blade slicing through my skin. In my mind, the blade is calling to me, but I can't do it, I won't. I crawl under the covers of my bed, and bury my head in the pillows which still hold his scent. More tears fall for a man I could only ever have in my dreams.

I wake to the sun streaming through the French doors which lead onto a small balcony attached to my room. I groan when I realize; I had forgotten to pull the blinds closed again. It has been two days since I last spoke to Antonio. He sits in his car in front of my place or the cafe. He has tried to talk to me several times since I sent him away, but I don't know what to say. So, I say nothing. I know I have hurt him, but it's better to hurt him a little now, than a lot later.

Throwing the covers back, I climb to my feet and stretch before heading to the bathroom. Staring at the mirror, I'm not surprised to see my exhausted reflection peering back. Bags under my eyes, hair a mess. I know Brooklyn is worried sick about me because I haven't been myself lately. I vow to myself, today that will change. Stripping out of my pj's, I jump into the shower and allow the water to wash away the last couple of days. I need to be me again. I need to be strong. And, I need to convince Brooklyn; I don't have a care in the world.

After drying off, I wrap a towel tight around me and head for the closet knowing exactly what I need. After finding what I want, I lay it on my bed. *This will do nicely.* I turn and grab a belt off the back of the door before pausing and looking toward my dressing table to read the many post-it notes I have stuck to the mirror. I allow the words to soak into my bones, giving me the extra confidence I need to pull myself together.

You got this!

No Matter how hard it seems, push through.

You ARE beautiful.

You are Strong.

My eyes land on the one Antonio added when he was here and I feel my eyes glaze over with tears, I will them not to fall. I have cried enough over the past couple of days to last me a lifetime.

You were made for me

Pushing the tears back, I grab my belt and get ready for my day.

God, I feel good when I'm ready and I stand in front of the mirror. My black high waisted skirt ends just above the knees is matched with a black belt and a tucked in, green off the shoulder shirt. My hair is up in a 50s style, small strands curl around my face. Makeup is done perfectly with a splash of red on my lips. I smile to myself, pleased that I'm trying to be more like me again.

I bounce down the stairs and head toward the kitchen where I flip the kettle on and press the remote for background noise from the television. *I might drink coffee out the back today, it's such a nice day and I feel great.* Once the kettle boils, I make coffee and turn toward the back door. As I'm about to move, something catches my attention on the screen.

I gasp loudly. "Holy Shit!" I almost drop the cup of hot liquid to the floor. After setting the cup on the bench, I turn and head toward the stairs. I need to grab my bag from the bedroom. I grab my phone and replay what the news reporter had announced - *Darren Jacobs found dead in a car fire.* Fuck, that's bloody awesome, I want to dance about. Grabbing my keys, I hurry to the front door. I need to see Brooklyn and find out if she has heard the news. Evie hugs may help lift me a little too.

Antonio

Resting back in my seat, I stare through the

windshield of my car toward the French doors which lead into Kat's room. It's only been a couple of days since I held her, but fuck it feels like forever. I'm so fucking confused as to what actually happened to cause her to push me away like she did. But, whatever the issue, I *will* find out. I'm a man who doesn't accept being told no very well, especially when it comes to something I want. And, I want Kat.

As a young boy, I spent far too many years being told what to do, the only one I take orders from now is my boss, and best friend, Dominic. I would give my life to protect him and his family and I know he would do the same for me. He has been there for me through some of my darkest moments and I will be forever in his debt. I focus back on the doors and notice a slight shadow pass by them. What I wouldn't give to be up there with her.

I drag my fingers through my hair, slide the hand down the side of my face, feeling my two-day growth. I'm feeling frustrated that shit has to be this way, but know if I push her, she is more likely to withdraw even more than she already has. *Fuck. What the fuck happened?* Everything was fine one minute, the next I'm getting the cold shoulder as if what we shared meant nothing, I shared a part of myself with her, a part I have never shared with anybody else. *Did I scare her off?* Fuck, she should know I would never hurt her. I don't understand, she was fine after I told her what I did for a living and who Dominic was. Not knowing is driving me fucking crazy.

We were in her kitchen when I explained I was the *Capo Bastone* and I was pretty much the enforcer for the mob. She didn't act differently toward me, but it's not like we really had time to discuss it in detail. Dominic had rung and told me to get Kat and bring her over to Brooklyn's, someone had thrown a brick through Evie's window. That was the night she first let her guard down with me and finally gave into what was happening between us. I remember the way she tasted, the way her body moved against mine, begging for everything I had to give. I gave her every piece of me and saw in her eyes, she felt everything I did. It was the first time in my life, I had actually understood what making love was all about. *Fuck. How can I let her go after that?* I'm not. I fucking won't. I'll give her the space she needs, for now, but we are far from done.

"Holy Fucken shit," I whisper when I see Katherine step through her front door. I suck in a deep breath and grip the steering wheel tighter as I take her in from head to toe. My cock hardens instantly. She looks like something out of a wet dream. Her skirt is hugging her curves like a second skin, fuck. She looks like one of those women from the old retro drink signs. It is taking everything in me to stay put, to not rush over, push her back inside the house and claim what is mine.

Kat looks straight at me and I see the pain in her eyes before she turns away and heads to her car. *Where the fuck is she going dressed like that?* I have never questioned if she pushed me away for someone else, but right now the possibility of giving herself to some other fuck wit, has me on edge. I know I'm fucked up, and probably don't deserve her, but nobody else will ever worship or love her as much as I will.

She is mine.

Chapter Two

Katherine

Jumping in my car, I start the engine and try to ignore the fact Antonio is following me. I turn the stereo up just as *I Want to Break Free by Queen* comes on. I soak in the lyrics, trying not to think about the pain I had seen in his eyes when I came out of the house. I had to quickly turn away so he wouldn't see the tears filling my eyes. Winding the windows down, I try to get lost in the music as the fresh morning air washes over me.

I drive up the long driveway to the front steps of Dominic's place and glance around at the manicured lawns and beautiful picture windows. It's like stepping into a different world when I'm here. As I shift the car into park, *I Was Made for Lovin' You* by *Kiss* starts to play. I reach out, turn the car off and groan. Leaning forward, I bang my head against the steering wheel. *What the hell was that?* It's like even the radio station is trying to say something to me. *Fuck. Pull it together, you got this.* Serves me right for listening to the classic station.

I straighten myself, take a deep breath and flip the visor down to check my lipstick. That's when I notice Antonio sitting in his car behind me. *Shit I hope he didn't see my little performance.* Stepping out of the car, I keep my back to him as I hurry up the steps and knock on the door. I sense him move up behind me and freeze as he puts his arm out. For a moment, I think he is going to touch me but instead he reaches for the door handle and opens it. I breath in and inhale his scent. I catch myself leaning a little toward him. Pulling back, I take a quick glance at his face but he's not looking at me, his eyes are on the ground and I feel a pang in my heart knowing this is the way it has to be. Pushing my shoulders back I take a step forward.

"Kitten," he whispers and reaches out.

I hurriedly take another step and head inside before he has a chance to touch me. Fuck what would I do if he touched me? A shiver prickles my skin before I make a beeline toward the living room. Brooklyn is at the kitchen bench and I head straight for her.

"Something smells good, Dollface."

Taking her eyes off the bowl where she is mixing something, she looks up and gives me a bright smile. "Kat, wow you look amazing."

"You don't look too bad yourself, Dollface."I step

around the bench and give her a big hug

"Thanks, I feel great actually. It's as if a huge weight has been lifted off me, like I can finally breath again."

"I guess you've seen the news?"

Nodding her head, she stares through the glass doors with a smile on her face. I turn to see what she is looking at and notice Evie playing in the pool with Dominic. I turn back to Brooklyn and notice the shadows which usually dim her eyes are no longer there.

"I'll just head out outside." Antonio's deep voice comes from behind me and it runs through my body like a high voltage live wire.

"No worries, I think Dom wanted to talk to you." Brooklyn answers him before giving me a funny look.

I head to the sink and wash my hands, giving myself something to do.

"What do you need done?" I throw over my shoulder, not ready to look at Brooklyn just yet. *I need a few moments to gather myself again.* He didn't even touch me, he wasn't anywhere near me how can his voice affect me this way? I remember the whispers in the dark when he thought I was sleeping, the way his voice vibrated through my body.

I'm drawn from my rambling thoughts when Brooklyn speaks. "Do you want to talk?"

I turn, lean back against the sink and sigh. I really do want to confide in her but I can't do it. I cannot unload my shit on my best friend when everything is starting to look up for her. I shake my head not trusting my voice to answer her.

"I'm not weak anymore, you can talk to me you know. We have been friends forever you can trust me." Her voice is low with almost a hurt edge to it.

"I have never thought you were weak Brooklyn and I know I can trust you."

"I was weak. I should have left sooner. I should have done something before it got so bad."

She wipes away the tears that have escaped and run over her cheeks. I pull her into my arms and we hug.

Stepping back, I lay my hands on her shoulders and give a reassuring squeeze. "You did what you thought was best in a shitty situation, I probably would have done the same as you if he had threatened my child. So, stop being so hard on yourself, it's in the past and you can finally start moving forward. Be the woman you should have been, the woman I knew was hidden beneath the fear, babe." I sniff a little and pull her back into my arms.

Tears slide down my cheek when she whispers in my ear not to be too hard on myself, and when I'm ready to let go, she will be there to help pick up the pieces. I move away and we both wipe the tears from our eyes as Evie bounces in with Dominic and Antonio hot on her heels.

Dominic rounds the bench and pulls Brooklyn into his arms at the same time Evie jumps into my arms.

"Hey Babydoll, been good for mommy?"

"Yes," she replies with a bright smile.

I glance toward Brooklyn as Dominic speaks. happiness warms my body with the way he cares for Brooklyn and Evie.

"Is everything ok, Angel?" Dom asks my best friend.

"Everything is just fine Big Man." She stands on tiptoes and plants a kiss to his lips. "Kat and I are getting things ready for lunch. I was thinking, it's such a nice day, maybe we could eat by the pool. What do you think?"

"Whatever makes you happy, Angel. Antonio and I have some business to go over and a few issues to sort out, then I'm all yours."

"Oh, I like the sound of that." Brooklyn laughs as Dominic pulls her into his arms tighter.

I tune out the rest of their conversation, as much as I love seeing Brooklyn happy it hurts knowing I could never have what she has. I glance toward Antonio, he's leaning against the wall staring straight at me. I look away and hug Evie a little tighter in my arms.

"Hey Babydoll, do you want me to help you get some dry clothes on?"

Evie nods her head into my shoulder and in a small voice asks, "Aunty Kat, why were you and mommy crying?"

"Oh huni, they were happy tears, I promise." I kiss her forehead and head toward the stairs.

Antonio

I lean against the wall watching Kat. My eyes are drawn to her, she is an absolute vision even with tears in her eyes. I was relieved when she pulled into Dominic's driveway because I would have probably ended up in jail if she'd actually been going to see another guy. When I parked the car and saw her rest her head on the steering wheel as if in distress, it took every ounce of control I had to stay put. This is going to test my patience, but I'm going to try my fucking hardest to give her the space she says she needs.

I notice the small plaster on her wrist, and I'm hoping to Christ it's an old one. I can't bear the thought of something happening to her, I need her here with me. She probably thinks because the plaster is under her watch band that no one will notice, and maybe they won't, but I do. I notice everything about her, from the way her hips swing as she walks, to the sway of her hair. I know when her smile is fake and when it's real, the way it reaches those sky blue eyes of hers. I'm startled from my thoughts when Dominic calls my name.

"Antonio."

"Si Boss."I nod and follow him to his office, close the door behind me and take a seat in front of his desk as he heads to the bar.

"Bevenda,"(drink) he holds up the scotch in his hand.

"Si grazie."

I accept the glass he hands me, take a welcoming sip and relish in the familiar burn as it slides down my throat. I'm happy I'm actually able to feel something, instead of being numb and feeling nothing at all.

"Looks like you needed that brother."

I nod because I don't know what to say. How can I begin to explain something when I don't have the slightest clue as to what the fuck happened? Dominic doesn't question my silence but pulls out a file and slides it across the desk toward me. I pick it up and flick through the pages.

"Johnny called me this morning." Dominic takes a gulp of his drink and frowns. "Joey beat the shit out of one of the Chinese's women. I can't believe the stronzo has the balls to do it and still call himself part of our family. He knows how I feel about the abuse of women. He knows I don't tolerate it. You need to track him down and deal with him for good. I want him gone, understand?"

"Fuck, si I understand. But, what's this guy got to do with it?" I hold up the file in my hands.

"Theo tracked him down this morning as the last known person to have contact with Joey. I want you to find him and if he doesn't give you what you need take him to the docks."

I nod before standing and drink the rest of my drink. After placing the glass on the bar, I turn and head for the doors, pausing when Dom calls out.

"Capo Bastone, I need it done today. We don't need the extra shit going on right now. And while I think of it, now that piece of shit Darren is dead, we can ease back on the security on Katherine."

My stomach twists at the thought of not being close to my Kitten anymore, but maybe it's for the best.

"Si Boss" I nod and head toward the kitchen where I hear laughter coming from the girls. I pause in my tracks, there is no point going in there so, I turn and head for the front door. I need to get this shit sorted out and maybe that will give Katherine enough time to? To what? I don't fucken know.

Chapter Three

Katherine

Dear Diary,

It's been three weeks since I have seen Antonio, three whole weeks since he walked out of Dominic's house without so much as a goodbye. At first, I thought maybe it was for the best but now I'm not so sure. God, I miss him, but I keep telling myself to be strong and he is only doing what I asked.

So why do I feel so alone?

Every day it seems I struggle even more.

I hold the blade to my wrist every morning, praying

for the strength not to use it. Today I failed. I held the blade to my skin until a single drop of blood slid into my palm, tears streamed down my face. I was in two minds about what to do, I was so determined to keep going but something was holding me back.

It's like an endless cycle.

Every morning when I rise, I try not to look in the mirror. It will only justify in my mind, there is no-one to miss me.

I hate myself.

Every day is a battle, trying to convince myself, I don't miss him.

I try to convince myself that I don't look forward to seeing him, even if it's only a glance.

I wish I didn't have to battle these demons every minute of my life. I wish the past would stop clinging to me like an old coat.

I don't want to look back and dwell on things I can't change, but no matter what I do, it's always there tapping me on the shoulder.

I read a few other entries earlier to remind myself why Antonio is better off without me.

I am Broken. Every day I feel like I die a little more.

I place my Diary on the nightstand beside the bed and look around my bedroom hoping to find answers as to why I keep feeling like this.

The walls are beginning to close in on me, little by little, inch by inch. I need to get out of here and go for a walk, clear my head. I peer through the French doors, it's nearly sunset.

-------~●● ●●~-------

Gazing out over the water, I breathe in the fresh evening air. It's like a soothing balm to my soul, I don't have the weight of the world on my shoulders out here.

I draw in another deep breath and wrap my arms around myself, there's a slight chill and light spray off the water in the air. I love this time of the evening; the sun is setting and the light on the old lighthouse flashes to life. I wriggle my toes in the sand and listen to the waves crash over the rocks. A couple of surfers dot the water, sitting on boards bobbing on waves. They are mesmerized by the colors of the sunset. It's peaceful.

I sense him before he speaks, his energy surrounds me when he is near and a calm washes over me. I stand and turn to find Antonio watching me. He's behind me, all 6'3" of him, wearing black jeans and a gray fitted shirt. My eyes rake over his body and I hate that the first thought which pops into my head, is of how much I have missed him. His dark hair looks dishevelled, and needs a good cut, his face is sporting close to a full beard.

I gaze into his eyes; the color reminds me of the whiskey he likes to drink. My eyes travel down to the tattoos climbing both arms. My stomach twists and I want to run into his arms, feel the warmth of his body, but I force myself to stay put.

I can't give him what he needs, he has to move on. Wrapping my arms around myself a little tighter, I bow my head. If I look into his eyes again, I know I will see the hurt there and break. I summon all my strength, I have to do what needs to be done. I can't hurt him any more than he already is. I suck in a deep breath and start to walk past him, but stop dead in my tracks when I hear the pain in his voice.

"Please don't walk away from me, Kitten. I don't think I can handle you turning your back on me again."

I stand rooted to the spot, my back is to him. He doesn't see the tears falling from my eyes and running in streams over my cheeks. *Just keep walking.*

"Katherine, please tell me what happened to you? We can work it out together?"

I shake my head, there is no working it out. It is what it is. "I can't," I whisper hoping he will leave me be, but I should have known better.

"You can, Kitten. Talk to me. It has been absolute hell without you in my life."

"It just won't work, Antonio, you need to move on."

I tried to hide the heartbreak in my voice, but I don't think I fooled him. I feel the warmth of his body as he moves closer, and then his arms wrap around me. I'm surrounded by his warmth, making me feel whole again, for the first time in a long time. Fuck, I want to relax into his embrace and let him in. I'm exhausted, tired of fighting my demons. I want to fall asleep in his arms and feel wanted. But, I hold strong and step from his arms.

"Don't," he starts to say before I cut him off

"I'm sorry," I breath out as the tears start to come faster and I quickly walk away. *Don't look back. Don't look back.* I repeat to myself. *Be strong, you can do this.*

I breathe a sigh of relief when I reach my car. My heart squeezes in my chest when I realize he hasn't followed me. A sob breaks free and I feel sorrow deep in my bones, having his arms around me just now, would be the last time he will touch me.

Starting the car, I will myself not to look back. But, I'm only so strong and sneak a glimpse in the rear-view mirror. He looks lost standing alone, watching, shoulders slumped, no easy smile, and then he turns his back and looks out at the ocean. I wipe away my tears, and try to stop more from falling. But, I fail when I realize I have left my heart on the water's edge with him.

Antonio

I can't watch her leave again, I have kept my distance for three whole fucking weeks hoping to Christ she would open up and talk to me. I won't give up on her. On us. I look out over the water as the sun finishes setting, wondering what else I can do to bring her back to me. I don't know what I was thinking when I wrapped my arms around her, but fuck it felt good. It was how we're meant to be. I feel my phone vibrate, reaching into my pocket and after pulling it out, I glance at the caller ID. Johnny's number.

"Si?"

"We found him."

"Who?"

"Tommy, the guy that saw Joey last."

Shit, I must be completely out of it. There was only

one reason Johnny would be calling me at this time.

"Bene, Take him to the docks."

Stuffing my phone back in my pocket, I crack my neck from side to side. It's time to have some fun. Unwind. Ditch some stress.

"Tommy, you ready to talk yet?"

I'm standing in front of this piece of shit who is tied to a chair, in the dimly lit room at the warehouse near the docks. Watching as blood oozes from the busted lip I just gave him.

"Fuck you, I ain't telling you shit!"

"Okay, have it your way then, cazzo."

I chuckle low as I stride over to the wooden table with my tools laid out, I run my fingers over the various knives until I reach the pliers. Picking them up, I weigh them in my hand, they'll do the job. I turn and stalk back to the piece of shit Johnny has brought to me, he was found in Kings Cross selling drugs to kids. Drugs to kids – something I detest. So, it gives me a great deal of pleasure to deal with this waste of space.

Standing in front of him, I reach out and grab his hand which is tied to the arm of the chair by the wrist. I pry his fingers open so I can get a good grip. Clamping the pliers to the tip of his nail, I watch his eyes go wide when he realizes what I'm about to do. He struggles violently, attempting to break free. I ignore his pleas and with one hefty pull, I rip the nail clean off. When he finally stops screaming, I ask him the same question. He's a stubborn fuck. After getting no answers, I finish with one hand and let him know exactly how far I will take this until I get the answers I want.

"I can do this all night long and once I finish with your hands, I might just start on your toes. Or, I can take you over there and have a little fun." I point over my shoulder to a small shower cubicle. "I can put your useless ass in there, turn the water on and use a machine which sends volts of electricity through your body. You'll be in pain like you never imagined. You'll piss and shit yourself, your tongue will swell, your dick will pulse out of control and you'll be begging me for death. Your choice, what's it going to be?"

"Fuck," he spits out, wheezing and gasping through the pain. "I'll tell you everything I know, please don't kill me."

"I can't promise anything, Boss wants you gone. You should know better than to sell drugs to kids."

Chapter Four

Katherine

Dear Diary,

She hides behind a smile that lights up a room, making sure no one would ever know she is in pain.

Every laugh is to hide the tears she wants to shed.

Her touch is soft, and her heart is strong. No-one would ever know every beat of her heart makes her feel lonelier by the second.

She goes to bed hoping to fall straight to sleep so she doesn't fall apart.

Her tongue is sharp because she tries to protect herself from the hurt others have caused her.

Every day she struggles to breathe through the pain so she doesn't let herself break.

When I look at her I see her pain, but I also see the love she has to offer. The day she breaks, I'll be there to pick up – Every. Single. Piece. I'll put her back together again, exactly the way she was. No, I won't *fix* her. The demons she has faced everyday have made her stronger because she woke up and pushed forward.

She is perfect, a fighter, a survivor and she is Mine!!!

I drop the diary letter onto the kitchen bench. I'm also certain who the author is but I have to double check. I run upstairs, grab the post-it note written by Antonio the last time he was here, and take it back to the kitchen. Placing the notes side by side, I trace the words with the tip of my finger. I knew in my heart they would match.

Fuck, I'd almost forgotten how sweet this man is and that is saying a lot considering what he does for a living. Reading his diary entry again, I absorb his words deep into my bones, into my very being. I need them more than air right now. I rub the back of my hand under my nose, sniffling as I read, tears threatening to fall. Fuck, what is this man doing to me? He affects me like no other. He is determined to bring me to my knees and crack me wide open. I feel a flutter of hope in my heart, a moment of hope. Maybe this could work. If I give him a chance, let him in, instead of breaking me, will he put me back together again?

The house phone rings tearing me from my thoughts. I step over, grab it from the cradle and bring it to my ear as

I walk back to the bench and look at the notes again.

I sniff.

"What's going on?" My sister's gruff voice booms through the phone and tears my attention away from the spell of the words written on the paper in front of me.

"Nothing." I try hard to hide the fact I was crying.

"Why are you sniffling? Have you been having another broken moment?" Her tone is snarky, it's a voice I know well and it causes a chill to zip down my spine. Hairs stand on end, goosebumps appear. I rub my free hand up my arm in an attempt to quell the feeling of disappointment, inadequacy which always comes over me when I speak with Ashley. She keeps talking, she doesn't wait for a reply, she's not really interested. "There's a solution for that you know."

"Hmm, I know." I glance at the knife block sitting on the counter. It's full of razor sharp knives and taunts me.

"Well either do it and put us all out of misery, or shut up about it. Fuck, you're so pathetic I cannot believe we're related."

I will the tears not to fall at her words. If she suspects her words have caused me to cry, she will spill more hurtful words.

"You know you're broken, not to mention the other thing making you unworthy for anyone. Who would want you once they find out you can't give them..."

I zone out, will myself not to listen. I need to be strong and not let her words hurt me but everything she is saying is true. The flutter of hope I had a few moments ago when I read Antonio's words is gone. I'm like a black hole, I

35

feel worthless.

I need to disconnect the call. I have to be strong and ignore what she is saying. I want Brooklyn. Oh, God, I need to make the pain she causes, stop. My finger shakes as I click 'end call' and her voice fades away. I know I will pay for hanging up on her, but I can't deal with anymore of her today.

Sliding down the cupboards in my kitchen, I sit on the floor, bring my knees to my chest and try to breathe through the pain. I will the pain and darkness to leave me alone, I don't want to feel like this anymore.

A sob breaks free and I bury my head into my knees as I cry hard. After a few moments, I reach blindly for the phone. I wipe my hand across my face until I can see the numbers clear enough to call Brooklyn's number. I try hard to contain the sobs that pour from me, I need to speak with Brooklyn, and I hope she can help me. I can't continue on this way, I have to do something.

When Brooklyn bursts through my door, I'm still sitting on the floor in my kitchen. I haven't had the energy to move and I don't give a shit either. My best friend has seen me at my worst when we were kids, she was there for me then, and I hope to God she is here for me now.

"Kat, where are you?"

"Down here."

Brooklyn hurries around the kitchen counter and finds me on the floor. She doesn't say a word, but sits next to me and pulls me into her side. Tears roll down my face.

"I'm ok," I murmur.

"Bullshit, I know you're not." Her voice is barely a whisper and when I glance at her, silent tears drip from her lashes. She doesn't say another word, but holds me while I fall apart in her arms.

Brooklyn never pushes me to open up even though I know it hurts her deeply to see me this way. Knowing she cares, hurts for me, helps me believe maybe I'm not as worthless as Ashley says. It helps me knowing, that despite everything, Brooklyn will always be there for me.

"Ashley called me," I squeeze my eyes shut as her words play on a loop in my head.

Brooklyn reaches over, gathers my hand and starts caressing the scars on my wrist. Her loving gesture causes more tears to fall from my eyes.

"Kat, I am here for you, I always will be. Nothing will ever change how I feel about you. I know who you are and what's inside your heart. You love hard, babe, and protect those you love like a tiger protects its cubs. But, sometimes, maybe every so often, you need to let me help you. Let me in. Let me always be the person you run to when you need someone, because if I lose you it would break me. You are my sister, my best friend and my lifesaver, so please, I'm begging you, let me be yours." Her words break on a sob, and my heart aches with the emotion of her words.

I have to try harder to shake this feeling of loneliness, it's bullshit, I'm not alone. I have Brooklyn. Now is as good a time as any to start proving to my best friend, I will try. I reach into my pocket and pull out the razor I keep there. Grasping Brooklyn's hand, I place it in her palm and close her fingers around it. It's my silent promise to try harder.

"I love you, Brooklyn."

"I love you, Katherine. Don't you dare leave me here alone."

We fall silent for a moment, oddly I feel lighter, like a weight has been lifted from me. Maybe carrying the blade around with me was weighing me down, giving me an out that I never really wanted. I suck in a deep breath.

Brooklyn speaks breaking into the sad quiet. "Can we please get off the floor now, my ass is killing me?"

We both erupt into laughter, the tension broken for now.

Antonio

Under the shade of a tree across the street from her home, I watch from a distance, hoping she doesn't see me. I see when she picks up my letter from the door mat. Things have been tense with us since the beach incident nearly two weeks ago. When our paths cross, we barely mutter hello or goodbye. But, I had to try again. I can't walk away. I need her like I've never needed anyone. She calms the storm inside me and makes my heart beat faster just thinking about her. I never knew I could feel this way after everything I have been through.

As I stood on the beach after she'd left and watched the waves coming in, I came up with a new plan. I know she writes in a diary, I have seen it on her nightstand beside her bed. I didn't read what was in it, I would never take advantage of her trust in that way, but I had a feeling the demons she fights everyday are in there.

If this was the only way I could convince her we are meant to be together, then I will take it. I'm not sure if it's a good idea or not, but I'm willing to try anything at this point. I thought if she saw the words, my feelings written down, then she would start to believe she doesn't need to keep everything inside. I can be the person she needs, to release and unload to. I can help her win the battle within. Fuck, I can help her win the fucking war. If what I wrote brings a smile to her face for five minutes and causes her to think about things, I will take it.

I'm not sure how long I stand staring at her front door. I'm not even sure what I'm waiting for, but I can't walk away. If this is as close as she'll allow me, then this is where I will stay. I hear the sound of a vehicle approaching and Dominic's black *Lexus* pull up in front of Kat's place. Brooklyn leans over and kisses Dominic, he shakes his head before climbing out and rounding the car to open her door.

Evie is in the back seat. I see what he has and a pang of jealousy hits me in the chest. I'm fucken pleased he is finally happy, but I can't help feeling pissed off that I can't have it too. How would it feel to be able to come home to Kat every night?

I stride through the front door of Dom's place later that afternoon and notice the changes Brooklyn has made including a large vase of flowers on the side table near the front door. The biggest change is Dominic himself. Yeah, he still believes his girls deserve better, but he will never let them go and he will do anything to make them happy.

When I enter the living room, I see Evie laying on the lounge, a movie with trolls plays on the television. Dom is sitting on the other lounge with papers scattered all over the coffee table in front of him.

Raising a finger to his lips, he stands. He indicates with his head to the glass doors leading to outside near the pool. I notice Evie is asleep, so I nod and follow him out.

"Antonio, thanks for coming over. I've been going over that scumbags file, the one you dealt with a couple of weeks ago, and I'm trying to figure out where the fuck Joey could be."

"Johnny has had eyes on the place Tom gave us the info for, but there's been nothing as yet. Theo is keeping track of his bank accounts, and Nico is tracking down his drug dealer. We're onto it boss, we will find him. The fucker can't hide from us forever."

He nods and looks out across the yard. "Good, I want this shit sorted. Until it's done Brooklyn would feel much better if someone was looking out for Kat. Do you think you could organise someone?"

"I've got it under control." I attempt to hold back my anger when I speak, because no-one, and I mean no-one is going to be watching my girl, but me. Fuck, Dom could have my balls for speaking to him this way, I'm not thinking clearly.

"Very good." He smirks at me.

Fucker, he knows how I feel. He knew how I'd react and knows I would never allow anyone else near my girl.

"Take care of it, I have to go grab Brooklyn from Kats place. She called me not long ago, Kat's been drinking, so she can't drive my Angel home. I don't know what I'll be walking in on, Kat can be rather feisty when she has a skin full." He chuckles before heading back inside.

I gaze out across the yard. I'm glad Brooklyn is there for Kat, but I'm also jealous. I should be the one with her.

Kitten *will be* Mine.

Chapter Five

Present day...

Katherine

A million thoughts are running through my mind at warp speed, Brooklyn, Evie, and the first time I met Antonio.

Antonio, a sexy Italian who caused my body to go berserk. It was like putting popping candies in your mouth, snap, crackle, pop. But, imagine that feeling crackling and popping throughout your entire body.

When he touched me, I felt it deep in my bones.

Everything finally seemed to make sense and I thought, maybe I could let him in a little. I knew he'd get bored and move on. To my horror, the complete opposite happened. Before I knew it, we were serious and moving way too fast. So, I did the only thing I know how to do, I pushed him away. These past two months without him have been fucking torture.

Every time I see him, I remember the last time he touched me, the warmth of his hand, the tingling feeling I had when he ran the tips of his fingers down the side of my face.

Every smile he threw my way caused my knees to weaken, but nothing compared to his eyes, the way they devoured each and every inch of me like I was the only woman on Earth for him. What I wouldn't give right now to be wrapped in his strong arms, to feel the softness of his lips as he presses them to my mine.

It wasn't right for me to hold him back from having a life filled with family. I knew I loved him, and as much as that scared me, I accepted it. But, I couldn't bear the thought of the disappointment in his eyes when I shared my secret. It would have broken me when he turned his back and walked away, and I knew he would. It would only have been a matter of time before he realized I couldn't give him what he wanted. He would leave and break me into a million pieces.

The damn man hasn't made it easy, he's been persistent and won't let me go. He's determined to bring me to the ground and crack me wide open, and this time I think I'll let him. I'm sick of hiding my feelings. First though, I have to work out a way to get us the hell out of here so I can finally tell Antonio everything.

⁂

I'm snapped from my whirling thoughts when I hear Brooklyn shout my name followed by a squeak.

"KAT!"

Lifting my head, I groan and wince with the throbbing in my cheek and the feel of the chains digging in every time I move. Brooklyn is on all fours with a chain wrapped tight around her neck. My chest squeezes at the sight. I blink a few times hoping to God I'm imagining this.

"Brooklyn," I wheeze out. "I'm... Sor-sorry" How the fuck did I let this piece of shit get the better of me? I remember leaving the house and heading toward Brooklyn's so we could head to the beach. I stopped at the café to grab my watch which I'd left in the kitchen when doing the dishes yesterday. I heard a noise coming from the front and thought it was Antonio coming to talk to me again. Question me.

After the letter, Antonio left on my door step, and me falling to pieces in Brooklyn's arms afterwards, I decided I was going to push harder to get better. But I wasn't sure if I was ready to let Antonio fully into my life again. Every day, since the first note turned up, I found another post-it note waiting for me when I walked outside. Written on them was one simple word, nothing more. After each gesture, the flutter of hope I thought had died, was slowly coming back. But, I didn't have time to talk to him at that very moment, I was already late getting to Brooklyn's.

"Antonio, I don't have time for this today," I call out

44

before making my way out of the kitchen.

"Katherine, Katherine, Katherine."

I freeze at the sound of the familiar voice grating down my spine and causing my heart to squeeze in my chest. I stare at the man, not believing what I'm seeing.

"Darren?"

"You took something from me, and I want them back."

"Not gonna happen, now get the fuck out." I glance around searching for my bag so I can grab my phone and message, Antonio.

"You looking for this?" Darren holds up my phone and steps closer, forcing me to back up into the wall. A sharp pain burns my face as he backhands me.

"You will pay for taking what's mine." Darren spits in my face, another sharp pain and darkness descends over me.

I'm not sure how long I was unconscious, but when I come to, my arms are wrapped with a chain, pulled high above my head and attached to something hanging from the roof. My eyes felt swollen and the pain in my face was excruciating. I lifted my head to see where I was. I'm in a dimly lit room; Darren is sitting on a filthy mattress on the other side of the room.

"What have you done?" I hope the fear I'm feeling doesn't show.

Darren laughs like a lunatic and gets to his feet. "What have I done? No, Katherine, it's what you have done. You deserve what comes next" He moves closer to me, smacks me hard across the face and stomps from the room.

I shake my head to get rid of the thoughts and attempt to concentrate on what is happening now. I close my eyes and relax my breathing. I need to either get us out of here, or distract Darren and waste time so Antonio and Dominic can get to us. I take a deep breath and focus on what this monster is saying now.

"Well ladies, I hope you're both comfortable?" Darren says with a twisted smirk on his fuck ugly face. "Now I have your attention; I'll show you your next big surprise." He sounds excited like a fucking a kid in a fucking candy store. I look around the room wondering what the hell he is talking about when a sudden brightness hits my eyes. I blink a few times so I can adjust to the light. Once the spots have vanished, I look around. My eyes widen when I see the newspaper articles pinned to the walls. What the Fuck? I suck in a breath and snap my head back to Brooklyn when I notice the one about her parent's death. Tears cascade down my cheeks.

"No," Brooklyn whimpers "No… no… no." She gasps, struggling to breathe.

My heart breaks for her and I sob. I need to calm her down otherwise, she'll pass out.

"Calm down, Dollface please, honey," I beg through my sobs

"Ah, I see you have noticed my most treasured piece. Don't worry, daddy went fast. Unfortunately, mummy dearest had a bit of fight in her, I showed her the error of her ways." He cackles like a hyena.

"YOU SICK FUCK! WHAT IS WRONG WITH YOU? YOU

ARE A PATHETIC EXCUSE FOR A MAN!" I spit out and wriggle, trying to free myself from these fucking chains, but they just keep getting tighter. Fuck this can't be happening. I would swear this was a horror movie if it wasn't for the pounding in my head.

Darren storms toward me and grabs the back of my hair, pulling it back hard and making me cry out. I feel the blade of a knife push against my throat and I whimper when I feel the sting of the blade as it's pushed into my skin. It's a sting I know so well, and I'm not sure if I want him to stop or keep going. I'm in a haze until I hear Brooklyn's broken please and I snap out of it. I need to be strong, I can't allow myself to fall into the black hole. I have to be strong for Brooklyn. I'm stronger than this. I repeat to myself.

"STOP! Please stop!" Brooklyn sobs "I'll do anything you ask, just please stop."

He releases my hair and takes the knife from my throat before stepping back over to my best friend. His eyes drag over her body as he looks her up and down. "Oh, I know you will, but first, we'll have some fun."

He laughs maniacally and glances between Brooklyn and I. I watch in horror as he slices off her dress leaving her in only her swimmers. He runs the tip of the knife in circles over her leg. I whimper when he pulls back and stabs the knife into her thigh. I tug hard on my arms trying to pull free so I can stop this, but they're fastened tight. Fuck. I watch as tears flood Brooklyn's face, I need to stop this.

"Fuck," Brooklyn hisses out when he pulls the knife from her thigh and blood starts to trickle down her leg.

"Dear, dear, dear, Brooklyn, what a dirty mouth you've developed. It must be the bad influence from that dirty, fucking mobster your spreading your whore legs for."

"When he finds us..."

Darren bursts into laughter. "I forgot how funny you are." He steps closer to Brooklyn and speaks menacingly. "Do you really think that Italian prick will find us? I hate to disappoint you, but nobody's coming for you. I've told you time and time again, nobody gives a fuck about you. I didn't even give a fuck about you." He begins pacing between Brooklyn and I. "You were a means to an end. You were my first and only fuck up and you had to go get knocked-up, didn't you? I guess at the end of the day you served a purpose with the head jobs you gave me."

"What the fuck are you on about, you fucking asshole? You fucking raped her!" I scream at him with as much venom in my voice as I possibly can. Every ounce of pain and anger I have felt over the past two months explodes from me in that one sentence. My heartbeat pounds in my ears as I let the anger out. Fuck, it felt good. For the first time in a long time, I feel alive.

"Hmmm, that was necessary, unfortunately. I had to show her how naive she was and still is. Her getting pregnant was never meant to happen and then when she refused to get rid of the thing. I was forced to make a choice. It worked out well actually because I needed to appear to be a family man to get a promotion so me and Matt could keep doing what we were doing."

"Matt?" Brooklyn gasps out.

Who the fuck is Matt? I don't know who this Matt guy is, but obviously, Brooklyn does.

"Yeah Matt, my friend you came onto at the party.

Well actually, he's my brother. We had to pretend to be friends instead of family when we changed our names"

What fucking party? Please don't tell me there is another piece of shit like him walking around.

"What do you mean, you had to change your name?" Brooklyn asks quietly.

"I don't have the time to talk about all this now, but after our parents died we had to live with our grandma. When we were old enough we changed our names so we could get a decent job and keep doing what we were doing."

"I don't understand?" Brooklyn says. That makes two of us. He's talking in riddles and we're only getting half the story. I glance toward Brooklyn; her expression is riddled with confusion. I turn back to the piece of shit.

The only response we get is him smiling and waving his arm around the room as if what he is saying should be obvious. Then, the smile is gone and he turns to face Brooklyn again. Skimming the tip of the blade over her other leg before pulling back and stabbing her in the side of the stomach. I watch her eyes widen and hear the blood-curdling scream that tears through her sending shivers down my spine. *Oh God, the baby.*

"I'll make you suffer, for what you've done." He grunts as he pulls the knife from her stomach and I have no other option but to watch the blood ooze from the wound. I pull on my chains, knowing I can't get free but I need to distract him.

"What did she do?" I yell. "What the fuck did she do? You're the one who threw a brick through her window and pushed her into Dom's arms. Tell me what she did wrong?"

He whips around and trails the knife down the center of my chest causing me to suck in a deep breath Feeling the cool metal against my skin, has my head becoming woozy but I fight to stay in the here and now. "What the fuck are you talking about, what brick?"

My eyes widen and I quickly look toward Brooklyn noticing the same look on her face. If he didn't throw the brick, who did?

"She had my brother killed!" He hisses in my face, making my stomach roil at the stench of his breath.

"How did she kill your brother?" I pretend I don't have a clue what he's talking about, but we both know he must have been the one in his car when it caught fire.

"Your brother was in your car?" Darren doesn't reply, he stares at the wall behind me. "So, you weren't stalking Brooklyn?"

"Oh, I was watching her, biding my time. Working out the right way to get at her, but then she met that Italian piece of trash which complicated things and I had to come up with other plans."

"But why, Darren? You never wanted me." Brooklyn sobs.

I notice her eyes getting heavy and her body sagging as blood oozes from her wounds. If it wasn't for the chains holding her up she would be on the floor.

"Because you decided to have that thing in the cage out there. While you were under my roof, everything was fine. Once you left, I couldn't risk you remembering what had happened that night and go to the police." He stalks toward her again. "You would have ruined everything Matt and I had going on. I couldn't allow that to happen."

"Tell me about this room, it must be important to you?" I'm trying to get his attention on me and away from Brooklyn. I watch as her eyes close and I whimper when Darren smacks her hard across the face.

"None of that, we still have things to do," he says causing my stomach to twist up in knots.

I don't like what he's saying, I need him to tell me about this room. How the hell are we going to get out of here? "All these articles you have pinned up, Darren, they must mean something to you. Talk to me." I persist, I'm not giving up yet.

"Ah Katherine, there's no need to be jealous. My attention will be on you soon enough; you have to wait your turn. You know, I've never had a redhead before." He turns to face me and starts running the knife down my chest again while licking his lips. I suck in a breath and try not to show him my fear, this piece of shit is not going to get the best of me. I glare into his dark eyes, daring him to do it. The sick fuck smirks at me as he whips his hand back and stabs me in the arm. "Arrgh,... You fucking piece of shit." I scream out and spit in his face. I fight against the pain, I will not allow it to overtake me and pull me into the dark place I know so well.

"Mommeee,"Evie screams out

Fuck no!

"Ah, the little bitch is awake. I think I may keep her around a bit longer than planned."

What does that even mean? I whimper again and struggle to break free, the chains dig deeper into my arms.

"Darren please let her go, she hasn't done anything wrong. PLEASE!" Brooklyn screams at his retreating back.

"No, I might go and say hello to the little darling," he tosses over his shoulder.

"NOOoo..." Brooklyn screams again but it breaks on a sob.

I scream out trying to get his attention, but it's no use.

A loud bang vibrates through the room as a door flies open and Darren rushes back in followed by one very pissed off Mafia Boss and right on his heels a very pissed off Antonio. I lock eyes with Antonio as he makes his way toward me. Hearing a loud Bang followed by a thud I turn and see Darren as he hits the floor. Thank fuck for small miracles.

I groan as Antonio lifts me into his arms and untangles the chains from around me. I allow my body to slump into his when I'm free.

"I got you, baby," he whispers into my ear.

"Please, don't let me go," I beg before breaking down in tears and burying my face into his chest.

"Never," he chokes out. I glance into his eyes and see the tears there.

Brooklyn screams and I turn to see her laying on the dirty floor in a pool of blood. So much blood, my heart skips a beat.

"Antonio, help Dom please, I can't lose her"

"It's ok, Dom's got her."

"Daddy!" I hear Evie scream. She pushes out of

Sergio's arms and runs full pelt at Dominic. "Daddy, I was so scared, but I knew you would come for us." She sobs against him.

"It's alright, Princess, I have you now." He kisses the top of her head, trying to hold her while applying pressure to Brooklyn's side. I watch as Brooklyn's lips move but she speaks so low I can't hear her.

"BROOKLYN! Don't you dare fucking leave me. I need you, we need you. Sergio take Evie now." Dom's voice borders on hysteria.

"Mommy." Evie cries out as Sergio picks her up and cradles her in his arms.

I look at Dom and see the tears pouring from his eyes.

"Antonio, I can't lose her... I just can't." I cry out when Antonio starts carrying me from the room toward the car. Sergio places Evie in the back of the car.

"Antonio, I want Evie with us, she *needs* to be with us."

Antonio

I can't explain the feelings when I walked into that room and found Katherine strung up with chains hanging from the ceiling, blood dripping over her fair skin. It was like I was thrown back into the past and I was a little boy again. Reliving the nightmare of the day I came home from school and found my momma laid out on the floor; beaten and bloody, curled up in the fetal position, sobbing as some strange man hovered above her doing up his pants and chuckling at what he had done.

I focus on Kitten and try not to think about that day, the day that changed my life forever. I wrap my arms around Kat and hold her closer. Evie is sleeping curled up in Kats lap as we wait in this fucking waiting room, sitting on uncomfortable plastic fucking chairs waiting to hear from a doctor about Brooklyn. I look toward Dom, my Boss, my best friend and the man I consider my brother. Tension rolls off him in waves and I know he won't be the same if Brooklyn doesn't come back from this.

"Boss?"

He looks over toward me, eyes full of worry. He paces like a lion trapped in a cage and ignores me.

I kiss the top of Kat's head inhaling her intoxicating scent of coconut and try to calm myself down. I hate that her scent of coconut is overwhelmed by the odor of that dirty place. But, it feels good to have her in my arms again.

"Antonio," Kat whispers and I lean back, gazing into her teary eyes "She has to make it, I don't know what I'll do if I lose her." She sobs hard and buries her face into my neck, her body shudders, and trembles as her soft sobs tear through her.

'Shhh Kitten, Brooklyn is strong." She nods and I pull her closer, relishing the fact she is not pushing me away. I have been lost without her for the past two months, not being able to hold or touch her has been fucking torture.

I'm not sure how much time had passed before the Doctor comes in holding a clipboard in his hands. He's an older gentleman with gray hair and he's round in the middle. He's aware of what happened and he knows better than to call the police. He has known our family Doc for years so he knows the drill. It's good, we don't have to worry about the legal shit, we can concentrate on Brooklyn.

"Mr. Grasso?"

"Si, how is she?" Dom rushes to ask as I get to my feet, placing my hand on Kat's shoulder so she stays seated.

She looks up at me with a scowl on her beautiful face. Fuck it's good to see some of the fire back in her eyes again. I nod my head toward Evie. Getting my meaning, she nods her head and looks toward the Doc.

"Miss Mackenzie has lost a lot of blood, but we have managed to stop the bleeding, and stitched up both wounds. Thankfully the knife didn't hit anything serious and she should make a full recovery."

I feel Kat's body relax under my hand on hearing the news and watch Dom sit, dropping his head into his hands, breathing deeply. He seems to relax until his head jerks up and his body locks with tension

"The bambino?" he chokes out.

"The baby is fine Mr. Grasso. Like I said before, the knife didn't hit anything serious. We have blood up to replace what she has lost and Brooklyn is currently being moved to a private room. When she is settled, the nurse at the desk will direct you where to go. She'll be sore and may tire easily for the next couple of days."

"Thank you, Doctor." Dom nods and shakes his hand.

"Mommy is ok?" Evie's sleepy little voice comes from beside me. And I look down into little blue eyes swimming in worry.

"Yes Princess, momma is fine and so is your little brother or sister," Dom reassures her, lifting her from Kat's arms and places her on his hip.

"I want to see mommy." Evie sobs into the side of his neck.

Kat stands and I wrap my arms around her, pulling her into my side. Thanking Christ, she is still here with me. Fuck, I don't want to think about the alternative. I suck in a deep breath and let it out slowly as Kat wraps her arms around me. She's safe, she's here and she's Mine.

"I'll go and check if she's ready for visitors." The Doc breaks into my thoughts and I watch as he turns toward the nurse's station.

"You do that," Dom replies tersely before turning and locking eyes with me.

"How about we go and have a drink while we wait for the doctor to come back and tell us where Brooklyn is, Kitten?" I nod my head toward Evie again.

"Sounds like a good idea, Come on Babydoll." Kat releases me, reaches out and gently takes Evie from Dom.

Chapter Six

Katherine

Following behind Antonio as he pushes through the door of Brooklyn's hospital room, I place a smile on my face and grab hold of Evie's hand. I don't want my best friend to think I'm not okay, she has already been through enough today because of me. I watch as tears stream down her bruised cheeks, and notice the IV attached to her hand. Antonio breaks my train of thought when he reaches for Evie and lifts her onto the bed before sitting in a chair and pulling me onto his lap. Brooklyn smiles at me through her tears and I'm not sure what to say so I just shrug my shoulders.

"Mommy," Evie speaks softly as she crawls up beside her. "I missed you so much."

I watch as Evie snuggles in closer to Brooklyn. Her mother strokes her back soothingly and assures her she's fine and isn't going anywhere. I glance toward Dominic and notice the love and relief in his eyes. My heart twists at the thought, I could have been the reason he lost them. I try to will the dark thoughts away, but it's hard.

Dom pats Evie's back. "Gentle with momma, Princess."

Evie pulls back and wipes her hand under her nose. "I'm sorry, momma."

Antonio nudges me, but before I can say anything, the door opens and the Doctor from earlier walks in studying the chart in his hands. "Oh, there's a full house in here." He smiles warmly at Brooklyn, but when he looks toward Dom, the smile leaves his face.

I notice the possessive look Dom is throwing the Doctor and the way he hugs Brooklyn closer. I bite my lip and try not to laugh. I catch Brooklyn's eye, she raises an eyebrow, that girl knows me too.

"Brooklyn, how are you feeling? My name is Dr. James Williams."

"I'm okay, a little sore but, okay."

"You will be sore for a couple of weeks and you may tire easily. I came by to check in with you and give you something for the headache you must have, it's safe to take these while you're pregnant. I also wanted to have quick chat about something if that's okay with you?"

"Is everything okay, Doctor?" I hear the worry in

Dom's voice causing me to shift a little on Antonio's lap, he pulls me in a little closer.

Fuck, it feels good to be in his arms again. I relax into him and a sigh leaves my lips when I hear him breath in my scent. I focus back on the doctor when he speaks.

"Yes, it's nothing to be alarmed about, I hope."

"What is it?" Brooklyn's voice is laced with worry.

I sit up straighter, worried about what he is about to say. Antonio rubs his fingers over my belly, trying to soothe me I guess.

"Would you like to talk in private?" The doctor asks Brooklyn and Dom.

"No, I want my family here."

Dr. Williams nods and glances at the chart in his hands before looking up again. "When you were brought in and we were informed you were pregnant, we gave you an ultrasound to check everything was okay with your child."

I rub the sweat off my hands on the spare scrubs the nurse gave me when we came in. Really not liking the sound of this, what if I caused her to lose the baby? What the fuck would I do then? How the fuck could I ever face my best friend again? Antonio rubs my back and I feel the tension start to leave my shoulders at his touch. But what if Brooklyn hates me forever? I don't think I could live with myself knowing I caused her to lose a child. I'm jolted out of my whirling head when I hear the Doctor's next words.

"I believe you're having twins. We can't be one hundred percent sure this early in a pregnancy, and there are a number of other things it could be, but there's a good chance you are carrying twins. When the technician performed the ultrasound, she heard the faint echo of a second heartbeat and detected what could be the start of a second child."

All the air leaves my lungs in a whoosh, I look toward Brooklyn and notice her wide eyes. Turning to Dom, I see the huge grin on his face before he kisses the ever-loving shit out of her. She starts to ramble when he pulls back and Dom chuckles.

"I'm going to have two brothers!" Evie squeals and bounces on the bed as she claps her hands. I move off Antonio and scoop her up so she doesn't accidently jump on her mother.

"Brother's? Two. Two boys. Maybe two girls. Maybe one boy and one girl." Brooklyn is still rambling on. We all burst into laughter. After Dom explains exactly why they are to only have boys, I can't help the laugh which slips free at the way he thinks. Antonio also bursts into laughter. I stop suddenly at Brooklyn's pained cry when she cups her side.

"Okay, Angel, that's enough excitement for one day. Time for you to rest now, my darling," Dom says.

"I want to go home to our bed?" Brooklyn pouts making me snort at the action. She so learnt that from me.

"I'll see what I can do after you rest here for a few days."

I place Evie back on the bed and watch as she crawls to snuggle into Brooklyn's chest, my heart twists again at the thought I could have lost them. I lean over giving her a hug and whisper in her ear "Congrats Dollface, love you so much."

"I love you too Kat, I'm so happy you're okay."

I take a step back and blink a couple of times to clear the mist which has formed in front of my eyes, willing myself not cry. How can she be happy *I'm* okay? Shouldn't she be angry and upset with me for leading that monster back to her?

Antonio leans over and gives Brooklyn a hug, Dom growls. Antonio leans back and raises his hands in the air. "Boss, she's like a sister to me." Wrapping his arms around my waist, he bends and kisses me gently. "I have all I'll ever need right here."

"Awww," Brooklyn says with mock sweetness.

"Shut ya face bitch"

Dom chuckles as he looks at Antonio. He nods. "Si, I understand, but right now, I think it's time for my girls to get some rest and then we can all head home."

Home, I like the sound of that, but it scares me a little as well. I don't want to be the person I have been for the past couple of months. It's time I came clean and bared my soul to the one man who insists we can get through anything as long as we are together. Fuck, I hope he means what he says.

Wishing everyone goodnight before bending over and laying a gentle kiss to Evie's forehead, we head out the door.

Antonio

We enter the hotel room Dominic organised for the

night and I glance around while I remove my jacket and drape it over the back of the chair in the corner of the room. It's not much to look at with a queen size bed in the middle of the room, a small kitchenette and a door on one side which leads to the bathroom. It's basic but enough for tonight.

"Why don't you go and have a shower, Kitten. It will help you to feel better." I nod toward the closed door. Kat looks at me then at the closed door. She's biting her lip as if trying to make up her mind about whatever is going through her head. Eventually, she turns and heads toward the door. Placing a hand on the handle she pauses and looks at me over her shoulder.

"Will you be here when I come out?"

I look into her eyes and see a thousand emotions clouding them. I can't pinpoint if she wants me here, but fuck if I'm leaving her alone tonight.

"Si." I give a sharp nod.

She nods and I watch as her body visibly relaxes as she heads into the bathroom and closes the door.

If she thinks I'm leaving she has a lot to learn, I gave her space for two whole fucking months and it just about killed me, I'm not waiting anymore. By the end of the night Katherine is going to realise exactly how this is going to go and that she is mine just as much as I am hers. The feelings running through me today just about tore me apart. Not knowing where she was, if I would ever see her alive again, touch her or listen to her smart mouth sent chills down my spine. And, not the good kind. I knew losing her would break me and there would be no coming back from it. I know the demons she is fighting are taking a toll on her, but if she thinks telling me will stop me pursuing her, she has a lot to learn.

"Antonio," her voice breaks through my thoughts.

I raise my eyes and catch her staring at me. I try to keep my eyes locked on hers, I really do, but it's hard when she's standing before me with nothing but a towel wrapped around her. Her hair is tied up in a messy bun and a few tendrils have fallen loose to gently frame her face. FUCKING GODDESS IS WHAT SHE IS! What I wouldn't give to be able to kiss and fuck her right now.

"Antonio," she says again and I snap my eyes back up to hers and notice the smile curling her full lips.

"Si, Kitten." I clear my throat.

"Would you happen to have a spare shirt I can wear? I really don't want to wear the scrubs."

Without a second thought, I rip my shirt over my head and step toward her. I slip it over her head, grazing the tips of my fingers down the curve of her neck, feeling her pulse pick up speed, and the slight gasp of air which escapes her lips. I draw in her intoxicating scent and take a step back in time to watch the towel slide down her legs and hit the floor. Slowly, very, very slowly, I let my eyes take in the sight of her in my shirt. Mine, Mine, Mine... is on replay through my mind.

"Fuck." I drag my fingers through my hair before turning away. I need to get myself together before I pin her to the wall and fuck the shit out of her right here and now.

Katherine

I love the way his eyes track every movement I make, my body zings and zaps at the way he looks at me. His scent surrounds me, and the warmth of his body still clings to his shirt. I watch as his tattooed muscles flex and the glint of his nipple piercing catches my eye. I lick my lips wanting nothing more than to play with it with my tongue, I'm broken from my trance with the sound of his husky voice.

"Fuck," he says before turning away.

I need to tell him why this won't work, if I let it go any further it will get messy really fast and I don't want to hurt him. I would rather he walk away now. But, I need him to look at me first.

"Antonio, I need to....."

"I need a minute," he cuts me off. Shit is he leaving me already and I haven't had a chance to tell him?

"Please talk to me, you need to understand why this won't work."

Antonio spins around faster than the speed of light, the slightest flicker of anger crosses his eyes but then disappears. "Why Kitten? Don't fuck with me this time, just tell me. I know you want me as bad as I want you. I can see it in your eyes. Tell me why you think it can't work."

Sucking in a breath I let it out slowly, and just spill my guts like he's asked me to. "I may never be able to give you a family."

"What do you mean?" He stares into my eyes and I almost lose myself in them for a minute. Clearing my throat, I go on.

"A Baby. Children, I may never be able to give you any."

He gazes at me with a look on his face I don't understand. He finally realizes what I mean and I guess my first instinct was right, he turns around and heads toward the door. My eyes fill with tears and I peer down at my feet, trying hard not to let the tears fall. I refuse to break down again over something I'd already anticipated. Fuck, I knew this would happen. I destroy everything I touch. I hear the lock click and let the breath go I didn't realize I was holding. With my arms wrapped around my waist and tears cascading over my cheeks, I remind myself again why I don't let anybody in. I raise my tear soaked eyes and gasp when I see Antonio leaning against the door with his arms folded across his broad, naked chest.

"Antonio?" He raises his hand and I close my mouth.

He's like a tiger slinking, stalking his prey as he crosses the room and stands before me. He sighs deeply. "How can you not understand I can't stop thinking about you? You're like an addiction I can't fucking shake and don't want to. That mouth of yours, with the things you say, you aren't afraid. You are like nothing else in my life." He groans and pecks at my lips. "I have never, and I mean *never* been pushed to the limit where I either want to kiss the fuck out of you, turning your words into moans. Or, tie your ass to my bed and fuck you so hard the only thing to escape those lips are pleas for more." He growls sending a pulse through my veins which causes my body to hum. "Do you finally get it, woman? You're a psychotic bitch sometimes but..." He kisses my lips as he speaks the words one by one. "I. Fucking. Love. You. So, you can keep trying to push me away, but I'm telling you now...."Again, with the kisses. "I.

Am. Not. Going. Anywhere! Capisce? You're mine, Kitten and that will never change." He raises an eyebrow at me, daring me to challenge his words.

Well I have a few words for Mr. fucking Romantic. "Did you seriously just fucking call me a psychotic bitch and tell me you loved me in the same sentence? You really are a piece of work you know that, Antonio?" I breathe out and slam my hands on my hips. I really want to be angry with him for calling me psychotic, but aside from Brooklyn and Evie, no-one has told me they love me for a very long time. Dropping my hands in defeat, I tell him again my worry. "But, I may not be able to give you babies." My voice is barely above a whisper.

"Kitten, I am not going to go over all this right now, it has been a long day and all I want right now is to lay you down in bed and hold you. I need to convince myself you're really here, safe and alive. I told you earlier, you are *all* I need. All I will *ever* need. The rest of the other stuff, we will work through together if and when the time comes. Maybe we'll adopt, maybe it will be just you and me. I'm a selfish bastard and wouldn't object to you being only mine."

"Okay." What the hell else do I say to that? "I love you too," I whisper before getting lost in his eyes again as his lips claim mine in a soft kiss, meant to tease and tempt.

"Come on Kitten, into bed you need to rest."

Rubbing my forehead, I notice the slight ache is still there. The cut on my arm and my neck are fine. I can't wait to go home tomorrow. After crawling into bed, Antonio hands me two pain tablets and a glass of water.

"Thank you."

"Always, Kitten." He takes the glass from my hands and places it on the bedside table before leaning down and kissing my forehead. I hum at the feel of his soft lips.

"I'm going to grab a shower."

"Mmmm," I murmur, already half asleep. I hear his soft chuckle as he walks toward the bathroom.

Katherine

Traveling home was long and tiring, but I was so thankful, the last thing I wanted was to be in Sydney for too long. Too many memories and not all good. I think the only good memory I would have was meeting Brooklyn. Antonio pulls up to the curb in front of my home, the home I once shared with my Mother and Grandmother.

My place isn't anything special but it's everything to me. It was built in the 1870s and I have keep everything original on the outside. The wrought iron fencing, a balcony on the second floor leading off my bedroom with intricate moulding around the windows and doors. It's had a fresh coat of paint in grays, and whites and the front door is a beautiful green to give it a touch of life. It's a cozy little place nestled between two other buildings. The inside has the living, dining, kitchen and laundry on the bottom floor. A beautiful staircase leads up to the three bedrooms and another bathroom. The thing about it I love the most, I have four fireplaces. Once winter settles in it doesn't matter where I am in the house, I can snuggle in front of a fire and read a book. It's my sanctuary, my safe place.

I'm snapped from my thoughts with the sound of a

car door slamming shut, I watch as Antonio rounds the hood of the car.

"Kitten." He holds out his hand and I slip mine into his and step from the car. "You might like to relax in a warm bath now the journey is over." He wraps his arm around my waist.

"Sounds like a great idea." No sooner have the words left my mouth then I hear my name being called out. I snap my head up to where the sound comes from my front door.

"Katherine, good, you're home."

"Ashley, what are you doing here?"

"I heard you were hurt and came to check on you." She waves her hand in the air as if her concern is genuine but I know it would be a bother for her to be here.

"I'm okay, you didn't need to come."

"This is my home too, isn't it?" She sounds annoyed as if she has every right to be here. Before I can say anything more, her eyes graze over Antonio and she saunters up to him like she walking a runway.

"Well hello there, handsome," she purrs seductively. She runs her hands over his chest. What the fuck? "Are you going to introduce me to your friend, Katherine? I'm sure he'd like to know me." Her hands continue roaming my man's chest.

"I... oh... sorry this is Antonio, my..." I stop short not knowing what to say.

"Her boyfriend." Antonio plucks her hands from his chest and tightens his arm around me.

Ashley glares at me, then back at Antonio. The

expression on her face says she doesn't believe it. I know I don't deserve Antonio but I don't want to let him go again.

She recovers, gives him one of her blinding smiles. "Well it's nice to meet you, my name is Ashley. I'm Katherine's sister." She reaches out and runs her hand down Antonio's arm. What the fuck? Why am I not telling her to fuck off and not to touch what is mine? Why do I still believe, after all this time she may try to hurt me? I'm snapped to the present when I feel Antonio step behind me and wrap both his arms around my waist. I could kiss him right now.

When I look at Ashley, a look I don't understand crosses her face. Then again, I don't really know her to understand her. But, I didn't miss the slight flair of her nose at me.

"How about we head inside and see what there is to eat?" Ashley swings around and stomps back into the house.

"Kitten, come on babe you need to rest. Let me hold you and we'll watch a movie or something"

I nod not sure how to explain what just happened. Antonio grabs my hand and leads me into the house.

Antonio

I'm not sure what just happened, or what is going on between Kat and her sister, but I didn't miss the look on Kat's face when she first saw her sister. When I wrapped my arms around her, I felt how tight and tense her body was. When Ashley touched my chest, I saw the way Kat's nose flared and I was waiting for her to say something scathing. She didn't speak which is completely unlike her. Over the past two months she was never this quiet. Something is going on between these two and I'm going to get to the bottom of it because I think Ashley has the ability to badly hurt my Kitten.

Leading Kat into the house, we head toward the kitchen to where her sister is rummaging through the cupboards.

"What have you got here to eat?"

"I'm not sure, I haven't had a chance to do the shopping yet. I'm not hungry. I'll grab a glass of water and head up to my room and lay down for a while," Kat replies

"Seriously? It's not even three in the afternoon." Ashley glances at her watch before looking at Kat like she must be joking.

"I have had a big couple of days and I just want to lay down."

Ashley laughs and waves her hand around like she doesn't believe her. "Of course, I forgot how lazy you are. Go then if you don't want to spend time with me, I'll stay down here and keep Antonio company." She looks me up and down like she is picturing me naked.

Is this fucking bitch for real? Kat looks at me, then back at her sister wide-eyed.

"Scusa, I'm going to lay down and hold Kat. It was nice meeting you." I'm proud of my control and being polite when all I want to do is tell her to fuck off. I will be nice for my Kat's sake.

Ashley rolls her eyes and turns back to going through the cupboards ending the conversation. We have been dismissed. Thank fuck, I'm not sure how long I would be able to hold my tongue if she continued being rude to my woman.

"Come on, babe let's get you up to bed. You've been through more than most people could have handled." I couldn't resist one dig at Ashley. Grasping Kats hand, I lead her toward the stairs.

"Sorry about her," Kat whispers as we make our way toward her bedroom.

"Don't worry about it, Kitten."

Chapter Seven

Katherine

Laying in Antonio's arms again makes me feel like I belong. I can't believe I survived for two months without him. Not seeing him every day, or feeling his touch, was slow torture and I guess he wasn't doing any better. I really believed I was doing the right thing for both of us. He insists all he needs is me, but what if he changes his mind and wants what I probably won't be able to give him? Or, that dark hole tries to drag me back down. What would he do then? I have always wanted to be a mother, to be able to grow a life inside me and give it life would be a dream come true but unfortunately, I may not have that option. I guess that's why I treat Evie like my own, I hate the fact I missed a lot of her growing up, but I can make up for lost time now with her and the new babies. I have never confessed to Brooklyn I may never be able to have babies. Trust me I wanted to, but when she got together with Dom and they were trying to get pregnant, I didn't think it was the right time. Then, when she found out they were expecting, I didn't want to be the person to rain on her parade in a sense. I don't want to be the kind of friend who takes a special moment away with a Debby downer moment.

"Kitten, what are you thinking about?" Antonio murmurs in my ear before he plants a soft kiss to my temple. "How are you feeling?"

"I'm okay. I still have a slight headache but otherwise I'm fine." I roll over so I'm facing him and snuggle into his warm chest. I run my fingers over his chest tracing his tattoos before finding his nipple bar and playing with it. I feel his body shudder and hear him draw in a deep breath. He places his hand over mine to stop the movement.

"Babe, don't start something you can't finish." He raises his eyebrows and has a sexy smirk on his face.

"Who said I couldn't finish it?"

"Kitten, you have been through a lot in the last forty-eight hours, you need to rest and let me hold you." His hand caresses my back. A yawn breaks free from my mouth making Antonio chuckle.

I glare at him not liking the fact he is right.

"Don't look at me like that, you need your rest tonight, babe."

I start to pull away feeling rejected but Antonio isn't having any part of that and pulls me back to him tighter.

"Don't be like that, I would like nothing more than to slide into your warm, wet heat but there is plenty of time for that once you have rested. I want you to relax and rest for tonight and we will see how you feel tomorrow, si?

I snuggle into his hard chest knowing he is right, not that I'd admit it. I lay my head on his chest and let his slow breathing lull me into a deep sleep.

Antonio

Laying here holding Kat in my arms gives me a sense of peace I haven't felt in a long time. I hate the fact she has been hurt and thinking about it makes me want to rip that piece of shit apart, knowing he is already dead has me feeling a little bit better.

I must have dozed off when I hear my phone buzzing. I glance at Kat and notice she has wrapped herself around me, it makes me smile to know, even in her sleep she needs me like I need her. It makes my cold dead heart beat a little faster, what I wouldn't give to wake up like this every day. Looking over at the clock, I note it's nearly 8pm. I reach for my phone.

Boss: Need you at the house Now!

Me: On my way

What the fuck could have happened now? Haven't we dealt with enough shit over the last couple of days? Slowly I slide out of Kat's hold, bend down and grab my shirt from the floor. I stand staring at Kat for a bit before placing a kiss onto her forehead and heading for the door.

"Where are you going, Stud?"

I stop and turn at the sound of Kat's sleepy voice and smile at the nickname she hasn't said in what feels like for fucking ever. "Dom needs me babe. I'll be back, I promise."

"You're leaving?" She sits up quickly and I notice she winces at the sudden movement. When I look into her sky-blue eyes, they are swimming in fear. What the fuck is causing her so much fear? I look behind me but all I see is the closed door.

"What is it Kitten?" I feel tense waiting for her reply.

Biting her lip, her tear-filled eyes bounce from the door to me to the floor.

"Kitten, I promise I'll be back." I try to reassure her but I'm so fucking confused about what just happened. Darren's dead, he can't get to her now so, what the fuck?

"It's okay. I thought you were staying the night."

I know she isn't telling me something but I don't have time to figure out what that something is, I have to go. I make my way back to the bed, sitting beside her I run my fingers down the bruise on the side of her face.

"I'll be back shortly, then you and I are going to talk about what is scaring you, si?"

I lean down and press my lips softly to hers. When I attempt to pull back, she wraps her arms around my neck and deepens the kiss.

I grip the back of her head and run my tongue along the seam of the softest lips I have ever tasted. I groan in the back of my throat at her taste, wishing I had time to strip her bare and fuck her hard and deep. My cock hardens painfully at the thought, trying to punch through my jeans. Pulling back, I rest my forehead against hers as we catch our breath "Fuck, I love you Kitten."

"I love you too, Stud."

Closing my eyes, I let her words wash over me. Words I have been wanting to hear for a long time. Opening my eyes again I look into the most gorgeous blue eyes I have ever seen. "I have to go, Kitten"

"I know," she nods biting her lip.

"Try and get some sleep and I'll be back before you open your eyes again." I kiss her one last time, get to my feet and head out the door. Fuck I love that woman. I make my way downstairs and stop with my hand rested on the handle of the front door when a voice penetrates my thoughts.

"Hey good looking, when you get bored with my sister, or when you finally realise what a waste of space she really is, don't hesitate to come knocking on my door."

I'm fucking pissed she would say shit like that about her own sister.

"Not going to happen, bitch. I love that woman upstairs you'd do well to remember that." My hand squeezes the handle as I fight to control my anger.

She narrows her eyes at me but doesn't say anything else. She storms away, back to the kitchen I guess. I need answers about this bitch from Kat but I can't ask her now, I don't have time, I have to find out what Dom needs.

Easing up the long drive to the front of Dom's place, I notice Docs car parked off to the side. What the fuck is going on? After parking the car, I hurry up the front steps and head into the house.

"Boss!" I call out.

"Si, Antonio, in the living area."

Hurrying to the living room, I stop short at the sight before me. A woman's body lies flat on her face with a pool of blood surrounding her.

"Janet decided it would be a good fucking idea to break in and aim a gun at me, but she didn't anticipate Angel shooting her first." When Dom speaks, I swear I hear a hint of pride in his voice.

"How the fuck did she get in here?"

"Apparently, she stole the keys off Joey"

I raise my eyebrows not understanding how the fuck Joey is involved in all this.

"Janet threw the brick through Angel's window to try and scare her off because she was convinced I was hers. When that didn't work, her and Joey organised for him to run us off the road. That didn't succeed so she came here to tell me I was hers and if she couldn't have me then Angel couldn't either. She pointed a gun at my fucking chest and was about to pull the trigger but my Angel beat her to it." He runs a hand through his hair.

"Fucking hell I knew I should have dealt with that piece of shit properly the last time I had him. I didn't think he would have the balls to do this shit. Fuck! What do you need me to do, Boss?"

"I need you to find that stronzo already, but when you do, call me straight away. You can have your fun but the end prize is mine." Dom's voice is deathly low and I know he means business and he's not to be fucked with.

"Si, Boss," I nod. "If you're okay why is Doc here? Are your girls okay?"

"Si, but Angel tore open some of her stitches." He runs a frustrated hand through his hair and blows out a deep breath.

"Brooklyn will be fine boss, she's a tough woman."

"I fucking know that," he growls and then shakes his head. "Scusa, Fratello it's been a long couple of days."

I nod my head understanding exactly what he means. "Boss, why don't you go and take care of your girls? I'll get the men to come in and clean this up and then we can finally track down where this fucker is."

"Si, call me when you get something, I want this sorted. This fucker should have been done away with already" He heads toward the stairs.

Pulling out my phone I dial Nico's number.

"Si, Antonio."

"I need you at the Bosses place, grab Michael on the way."

"On my way." He disconnects the call.

I'm not sure what game Joey is playing but he has played his last hand. It's time he rested with the fish. When I find him, he is going to wish he was never born. Pulling Theo's number up on my phone I hit call, I'm going to need him to get all the information he can so I can track this fucker down.

Katherine

Trying to get back to sleep is useless, my head is pounding, my arm hurts, and my stomach is growling. Tossing the blankets aside I stand and stretch my aching muscles. The last thing I want to do is go downstairs and face my fucking bitch of a sister, but I need some pain meds. I gather my robe off the end of the bed, wrap it around me and head downstairs.

Walking into the living room I notice Ashley sprawled out on the lounge watching some stupid television show, not paying her any attention I head into the kitchen. As I open the cupboard door, I hear her footsteps come up behind me and inwardly cringe knowing there is no way to escape this conversation.

"What are you doing?"

"I'm grabbing some pain pills for my headache." I don't turn to look at her and hope it will end the conversation, but I should have known better.

"Did your boyfriend get sick of you already?" She snorts and I turn at the way she says *boyfriend*, like she still can't believe I have someone.

"No, his boss needed him."

"What kind of work does he do to be called at eight o'clock at night?"

It's not my place to tell her about Antonio's job and even if it was, I wouldn't say a word. She could cause him a

79

world of trouble if she knew. I shut my mouth and at my silence she continues.

"He probably said that so he could leave and hook up with someone much better then you." Her expression as she rakes her eyes over my body is one of disgust and distaste.

"Antonio loves me, he wouldn't do that." Just thinking about Antonio with another woman twists my gut into a tight knot. The look, that I'm not happy with that thought must show on my face and gives her an opening to spew even more shit.

"How do you know for sure? Do you really think anyone could care about you? Does he know you can never give him a family? Does he know everything you touch turns to shit? Does he know about how broken you really are?" She glances at my wrists and I turn away so she doesn't notice my eyes fill with tears and hope she will just stop talking. Yeah, no such luck. It's like my uncertainty and defensiveness adds fuel to her poisonous fire. "Does he know you are the reason your so called best friend was raped?"

I close my eyes trying not to let her words affect me, but it's hard knowing she is telling the truth and I can't prevent the sob which escapes.

"I didn't think so." She turns and walks away but has to have one last word. "Oh, by the way, Antonio your *boyfriend* is probably fucking some other chick right now and I wouldn't blame him, have you looked at yourself lately?"

I hear her footsteps as she leaves the kitchen and that's when I realize the death grip I have on the kitchen counter. I can't stop the questions from running through my head. Is Antonio fucking someone else? Why didn't Ashley ask why I was so battered and bruised. I know I shouldn't listen to her, and she is nothing but toxic in my life, but it's hard to think clearly right now. Swallowing the pain pills, I turn and head for the stairs feeling the black hole starting to pull me back in.

Ashley calls out as I place my foot on the first step. "Maybe, sister dearest, you should put us all out of our fucking misery by ending your pathetic life. No-one would miss you."

I grip the banister a bit tighter and let the tears fall as the truth in her words penetrates my already swimming brain.

Chapter Eight

Antonio

I draw the car into the kerb in front of Kat's home. I reach over and grab my jacket from the passenger seat. I've been trying to figure out where Joey could be. Theo has drawn a blank. Joey hasn't used any of his credit cards for a while and the last time he did was a cash withdrawal in Sydney around the same time shit went down with the Chinese. Nico is still trying to track down his drug dealer to see if he has been in contact with him and hopefully that may give us a lead. I also have Theo researching Darren's background. There are some things about him which do not make sense to Dominic, the boss thinks that now he is dead we may have a better chance at finding out shit we couldn't before.

I drag my fingers through my hair. I'm fucking exhausted and all I want to do is crawl in bed with my Kitten. I ring the doorbell, hear footsteps on the other side of the door and hope like hell it's my Kitten and not her stupid fucking bitch of a sister.

"Good morning, handsome." Ashley's whiny voice prickles down my spine making me feel like I've fallen backward onto a bed of nails.

Fuck. I step sideways to look past her shoulder, not wanting to look at the bitch. Then I feel her fingers run down my chest.

"Katherine is still sleeping, maybe I can do something for you? I can offer you much more pleasure and satisfaction than that good for nothing bitch."

BITCH? GOOD FOR NOTHING? She calls the love of my life a good for nothing bitch? My anger goes from zero to boiling at mach speed. I grab her hand and apply pressure to warn her, I think how easy it would be to break every bone but I don't hurt women, not even this stupid bitch, so I throw her hand aside and step into the house, pushing her out of my way.

"Don't you get it bitch?" I turn to look at her and notice she is in nothing but a green, see through lacy nightie. Fuck. I turn back toward the stairs before I really lose my shit.

"No, *you* don't you get it. She's no good for you, she can't even give you a family. She's broken and worthless."

I spin around and step closer to her. "Who the fuck do you think you are?" I hear a noise coming from upstairs and see the glint flash in Ashley's eyes seconds before she slams her mouth down on mine.

"What the fuck?" Kat's screaming voice cracks on a sob.

Fuck! I push the bitch off me and turn toward the stairs in time to see Kat's devastated face before she runs up the stairs. I hear the loud bang of her door being slammed shut. I look back to Ashley smirking like she is pretty pleased with herself.

"What the fuck is wrong with you? I swear, if you were a man you would be dead already." I turn and run up the stairs, she laughs at my retreating back. The fucking bitch is psycho.

Katherine

Fuck. Fuck. Fuck. What the fuck just happened? Was she saying goodbye to him? Did he stay here last night? Did he decide I wasn't worth his time after all and slept with her? Question after question invades my mind, each one confirming how worthless I am. Just when I thought I had found someone I could trust, a man I could bare my soul to, I find him kissing her. Of all the people he could have done this with, he had to pick my sister. I breathe deeply before I dash into my bathroom and grab my razor off the counter. Ashley's words from last night taunt me -*Kill yourself! You're worthless! No-one will miss you!* Tears stream down my face, I can barely see out of my eyes as I push the blade against my wrist. I feel it slide through my skin like scissors through paper and watch as blood runs into the palm of my hand. I am feeling euphoric when a loud bang echoes in my room and the bathroom door is flung open. Antonio storms in, snatches the blade from my hand and throws it across the bathroom.

"Get Out!" I scream through my sobs and run a hand under my nose.

"Not fucking happening." Antonio grabs a washcloth from the sink and wraps it around my wrist in an attempt to stem the bleeding from my wrist.

I try to snatch my arm back but Antonio's grip tightens and he pulls me into his arms.

"You are going to calm the fuck down and tell me what the fuck just happened and anything else I want to know!"

He places a finger under my chin and raises my face so I am forced to look into his eyes. I can see he's pissed off. *He's* pissed off! He kisses my sister and *he's* pissed off! I need to explain myself? I don't fucking think so, I'm not telling him shit. "After what I just saw downstairs, I ain't telling you shit so you may as well fuck off. I saw you kissing someone else, not to fucking mention it was my fucking bitch sister and, oh yeah, God only knows what else you two have been doing while you were together all night." I push from his arms. "I'm done. We're done. Go and fuck her brains out if you haven't done so already."

It fucking broke my heart to push Antonio away, but I have to be strong and start building the wall up again. The wall I had protecting me for so fucking long until he came along and started chipping away at it. How could I have been so stupid to think he was actually genuine and not just a slimy piece of shit? Antonio pulls me back into his arms

85

and shakes me gently.

"Listen to me Kitten." Antonio's voice is husky with emotion.

I don't care. "Screw you, and the fucking horse you rode in on, asshole." I try to push from his arms again. Fuck he's strong.

"Katherine, STOP!"

Katherine? Whoa, he never calls me by my full name. I gaze into his eyes and see pain mixed with anger.

"Stop this. Stop jumping to fucking conclusions. I didn't touch her. I've been gone all night and I'd just walked in the door. She heard you coming and threw herself at me and kissed me. I swear to you, nothing fucking happened."

I look into his eyes trying to judge if he's telling me the truth. Can I trust what he is telling me? I relax a little in his arms.

"Listen to me, kitten. I would *never*, hear me now, Kitten, I would NEVER fucking cheat on you. I thought I made myself clear last night. You are *it* for me, nobody else would ever compare to you. I don't want anyone else, EVER. Fuck, I have never laid out my feelings for anybody before you. I love you, you have my heart. Nothing and nobody will change that." He looks into my eyes pleading with me to listen and believe what he is saying.

I want to believe him but.... but nothing. I should believe him, I can see it in his eyes, I can feel it in his touch, he's telling the truth. Ashley wants me to think Antonio cheated on me with her, to break me some more. I take a deep breath. "I'm sorry, I believe you. I love you."

His lips crash down on mine and he kisses me deeply.

"We are going to talk, Kitten, and you are going to tell me everything. *Everything,* including why your bitch of a sister wants to see you dead."

He waits for me to argue with him but I know we need to talk. "Okay," I whisper.

He sweeps me into his arms and sits me down on the bed.

Antonio

I return from the bathroom with a bandage in my hand which I got from Kat's medicine cabinet. I cross to where Kat sits crossed legged on her bed. I crawl onto the bed and sit in front of her, grab hold of her hand, remove the bloodied cloth from her wrist and begin wrapping it with the bandage. "Start talking, Kitten. I want the whole story. I'll know if you leave anything out."

"Ashley and I used to be really close but then our father left when I was thirteen. Something changed in her, she became abusive and physical toward me. I'm not sure what I actually did to cause it and when I would ask, she would tell me it was because I made daddy leave." Kat shrugs her shoulders and stares off into space. "When I was sixteen, she took me to a party. I left early but when I got home, mum was home from work, she'd left early. She asked me where I'd been and I told her the truth. When she knew Ashley had allowed me to leave and come home alone while she stayed, she became angry. Then, Ashley came home drunk. It was the last straw, they fought and mum told her we were moving back to Newcastle for a fresh

87

start. She wanted Ashley away from the party scene she was sinking into." Kat paused and gazed into my eyes, there was such sadness.

"As you can imagine, Ashley wasn't happy with leaving. She was having to leave her friends and her boyfriend at the time, I copped the brunt of her anger. I didn't blame her because I thought it was my fault. I'd caused it all to happen. If I'd been a good girl, our dad would have stayed and Ashley wouldn't have run off the rails. We wouldn't have had to move away. As I said, it was my fault and I had to live with it and try to be a better person. I built a wall around myself a long time ago, I needed to protect myself from the hurt. I only ever let Brooklyn in because she knew what was going on, she would let me hide at her place if things got too bad." She inhales a deep breath and blows it out. Tears sparkle in her eyes. There are a lot of issues in her statement which are completely wrong and they need to be talked about. Kat is blaming herself for things which were out of her control. I'll let her finish and then we will have a discussion.

"As we grew older, things seemed to get worse. She hates me, it's always the same with her. She says I should do what everyone wants and kill myself. I guess deep down inside, I'm still that scared little girl worried about what she thinks. I let everything she says get to me, I know I deserve her anger for causing daddy to leave. I ruined her life. She's right, I am worthless, maybe I should just kill myself."

I've heard enough. What twisted crap has Ashley been feeding her sister? I take Kat's hands in mine. "Kitten, first of all you don't fucking deserve to be treated like shit and second she has *no* right to blame you for things that were beyond your control. You didn't make her the way she

88

is, she did that herself without any help from you." I lift her chin up so I can look into her eyes and she can hear the conviction in my voice when I speak. "You don't owe her shit. She's a big girl with a lot of fucked up issues you shouldn't have to shoulder. If I ever hear you say you're worthless and should die, I swear to God, I'll.........Well, I don't know what I'll do, maybe I'll wring your pretty little neck."

"You don't understand Antonio *it is* my fault dad left and we had to move back here."

"How the fuck could it be your fault? Make me understand."

"The night my father left I heard him arguing with mum. The next day he was gone and when I asked Ashley why daddy left she told me it was because I was naughty and didn't listen to him."

FUCK! What the fuck did this bitch do to my Kitten? What kind of fucking sister would say something like that to their own sister? I'm trying to work out what the fuck to make of this. Something isn't adding up.

"Kitten, it's not your fault, I promise you. You were a young girl and it sounds like your father was an asshole for leaving, but what's worse is that bitch downstairs blamed you for everything. It wasn't your fault, darling, he made his own decisions to leave not you. You are a beautiful person with a good heart." I gather her in my arms and hold her while silent tears slide down her face. She may not believe what I'm telling her now, but I hope eventually she will understand it wasn't her fault.

"I'm not, I let Brooklyn down not once, but twice."

I run my hand up and down her back. "What do you mean you let her down, how did you let her down?"

"The night Darren raped her, I should have been with her but I got a phone call from the hospital telling me Ashley had overdosed. I had to leave and sign some paperwork."

I hold her back so I can look into her face. "Darling, did you know Brooklyn was going to be raped that night?"

"Of course, I didn't know, what kind of question is that?"

Kat snaps at me and I see some of her fire reassert itself. "A valid one." Before she can say anything else I go on. "You didn't know what was going to happen so what that sick fuck did wasn't your fault."

"But I should have been there. Brooklyn is my best friend, she has always been there for me. Instead, I was running off to the hospital for a sister who doesn't give a shit about me, to sign papers I have signed multiple other times when she pulls that shit. I let my best friend down for a piece of shit sister, how do I live with that?"

"Kitten, it wasn't your fault. You can't predict the future." I run my hand down her back and lay her down with me. She snuggles into my chest. I'm thankful she hasn't cut too deep and we're not sitting in a hospital right now. I kiss the top of her head when her sobs stop and her breathing evens out. I need to go and tell that bitch downstairs to get the fuck out and stay away from my Kitten but right now I need to hold her, and feel her. I close my eyes and try to erase the memory of her tear soaked face and the razor blade cutting into her soft wrist. Fuck, I need to get rid of that bitch from my Kitten's life. I take a deep breath, try to relax and draw my Kitten closer into my arms.

Katherine

I wake with a start and notice immediately, Antonio isn't lying next to me. Where did he go, did what I say earlier scare him off and he finally realised how screwed up I am? I hear a dish smash, darting from my bed I head down the stairs my heart pumping fast. What the fuck is going on? I pause when I hear Antonio's anger filled voice. I have never heard him so angry.

"I'm only going to say this once, Ashley. Get your shit and get the fuck out. Now!"

"Who the fuck do you think you are to tell me what to do?" The smugness in Ashley's voice grates down my spine like fingernails on a blackboard.

"You don't want to know who the fuck I am."

I can't take the shouting and head into the kitchen, I notice the pile of glass on the floor. "What the fuck is happening in here?"

Ashley spins around to face me. "Your boyfriend...."She makes air quotes with her fingers. "....thinks he has a right to tell me what to do in *my* fucking house."

I don't know what comes over me, but when I speak next, it's with so much menace in my voice, I surprise even myself. "This is not your house, this is *my* house and you need to leave. NOW!"

I watch as a stunned look crosses Ashley's face and she takes a step back. She recovers from the shock of hearing me speak to her with such confidence, straightens her shoulders and a look crosses her face I don't understand. She takes a step in my direction and it's my turn to take a step back. Fuck what did I just do? I feel a cold chill race through my body until Antonio wraps his arms around me. I relax into his hold and look Ashley straight in the eyes.

"This isn't over with." She pushes past us and storms through the front door, slamming it behind her. I'm not sure what she meant by that but I don't give a fuck either.

"I'm proud of you, Kitten." Antonio whispers in my ear sending shivers running through me and causing me to moan.

"How proud, Stud?" I feel his hot breath on my neck before a nip to my ear draws another moan from me.

"Upstairs now," he says in a commanding voice that gets my blood pumping.

Chapter Nine

Antonio

I round the corner to Kat's bedroom door, stop and lean against the door jamb. I study her as she sits cross legged on her bed staring through the French doors. *Fuck, she's Gorgeous.* What have I done in my life to deserve someone like her, I'm a mean fucker who hurts people for a living.

I clear my throat drawing her from her thoughts, her head snaps around, and two bright blue eyes focus on me. Pushing myself off the door, I make my way toward her. Standing before her, I watch as her eyes slowly lift to mine.

Reaching out, I cup the side of her face in my hand and run my thumb over her soft bottom lip.

"Fuck you're gorgeous."

She lowers her eyes to my chest and I miss the contact immediately

"Don't do that," I whisper. Lowering to my knees, I cup her face in both my hands, lean forward, and lightly graze my lips over hers. It's taking everything in me right now, not to smash my lips against hers, but I need for her to understand, I mean everything I say. I pull back a little and watch as her tongue darts out and licks her lips.

"Every time you take your eyes away from me I feel it here." I gather her hand and place it over my heart.

I hear her breath hitch and her eyes lift back to mine.

"I have spent too many nights without you, without being able to see your eyes on me. Now, I finally have you back, I need them on me, Kitten. Don't you understand what you do to me?" I blow out a deep breath before continuing. "The first time your eyes looked me over, I can't explain how much it affected me. It was as if I had found something, I didn't know existed. But, at the same time I knew I had found what was missing in my life. There's this black hole, right here..."I hold her hand a little tighter to my chest, but release it and run my finger under her eye to catch a tear which has fallen. "I realize now, I wasn't complete until that day I walked into the coffee shop and you looked at me with fire in your eyes. You set me on fire, I felt alive. I knew, if you could look at me for a split second and have me feeling that way, I wasn't letting you go."

Her free hand swipes under her nose when she sniffs back the tears. I notice the way her nose scrunches up a little, it's so damn cute. I can't help myself, I lean forward and kiss the tip of her nose before pulling back. I place my lips a breath away from hers and look deep into her eyes.

"Lay back baby." My voice is breathless and I notice her breathing increases as she shimmies backward until her head hits the pillow. I stand and look over her. I soak every part of her in, from her beautiful red hair sprawled across the white pillowcase and down her body which is wrapped in my shirt again. The sight has me holding back a groan. Reaching down, I adjust my aching cock and scowl when Kat giggles at my discomfort. Turning, I head toward the door.

"Where are you going?" Worry laces Kat's voice.

"I'm about to show you how needed you are, and you're going to lay there and take it."

I grab the black lace scarf off the back of the door and run it through my fingers, feeling the soft, silky material. *This will be perfect.* I glance toward my Kitten again. She swallows hard as lust flares in her eyes.

"Do you trust me, Kitten?"

"Yes," she answers with no hesitation in her voice

"I'm going to place this over your eyes."

"Isn't the purpose of a blindfold supposed to be that I can't see?"

I raise my hand to let her know to stop talking.

"I already told you, I want to *always* see your blue eyes staring back at me. I want you to know, it is me who has you begging for more." I wink at her, hoping for a smile. It's the next best sight in the world, besides her eyes.

Kat winks back and snorts as a smile curls her lips before informing me of just what she thinks of my statement. "In your dreams, Stud. I don't beg, Antonio. Ever."

I chuckle and raise my eyebrow at her. *Challenge accepted.*

Placing the scarf in the back pocket of my jeans, I pull my shirt over my head and watch as her eyes take me in. She licks her lips, and it sends a jolt through my body, causing my cock to punch at the zipper of my jeans. If I stand here staring any longer, I'm likely to explode in my pants. *Fuck, get it together, you fucking cazzo. What are you, a fucking teenager who can't control himself?*

Leaning over the bed, I run my fingers gently down the side of her soft face, over the bruise which has yet to fade. I pull back the anger I feel at her being hurt, and continue running my hand down over the swell of her breast, down her body until I reach the edge of the shirt. I plant my knees on the edge of the bed and run both my hands up her sides until I reach her neck, my finger grazes the small Band-Aid over a wound. Her body strains toward me. Grabbing the shirt in both my hands, I pull hard and rip it from her body, a slight gasp leaves her mouth. I bend down and kiss her lips.

Pulling back, she opens her mouth to speak, but I place my finger over her lips and shake my head. She nods her understanding as if in a trance.

Leaning back on my heels, I take in every gorgeous inch of her. Her full breasts with peach coloured nipples, pebble hard, begging for my mouth. I can't resist, and lowering myself, suck one into my mouth. I moan at the exquisite taste. Reaching blindly to her nightstand, I feel around until I grab what I want. Swapping to her other breast, I glance up and gaze into her eyes. They seem to have darkened with arousal. Releasing her nipple with a small pop, I lay a gentle kiss there, and then the other, so it doesn't feel left out.

I hold the feather, I grabbed from the nightstand and run it over her body. I watch the rise and fall of her chest as she squirms, her now sensitive skin responding to the gentle caress. I lean forward and blow over her puckered nipple, noting the light sheen of sweat forming on her milky white skin. I repeat the actions a few more times until she is writhing with want and small moans leave her lips. I stare into her eyes again, wanting her, no needing her, to realize this is more than fucking. I need her to understand she is mine and will always be mine.

"Beautiful," I note the flush in her skin, loving the slight pink tinge. Fuck, I love how her body comes alive for me. A whimper leaves her lips as I make my way down her body with the feather, followed by soft kisses. Her body arches for more, her hands move to her breasts and she fondles them, pinches and twists the nipples, tearing a moan from me. *Fuck, what a fucking sight.*

When I glance up, I find her eyes closed as if she is lost in her touch.

"Eyes on me," I growl.

Her eyes snap open immediately, my tone brooked no argument. I pull the scarf from my back pocket and place it over her eyes, just the sight about does me in.

"Fuck, keep your eyes on me. I need to see your eyes on me." I growl again. I struggle to control the need to mark her, and claim her as mine. What am I, a fucking caveman? My voice has become husky with desire.

Goosebumps break out across her skin and she nods her understanding.

I stand from the bed, unbutton my jeans, and draw the zipper down, allowing my cock room. It's getting fucking painful.

"Are you mine, Kitten?"

She nods again as her eyes take in the length of my body.

"Say it!"

"Yes."

"Yes what?" I need to hear her say she's mine.

"I'm yours."

"Whose, am I?"

Through the sheer lace, I see her blink a few times like she doesn't understand the question.

"Whose?" I lean forward and latch onto one nipple. I suck it into my mouth, sending the vibration of my voice running through her body. She moans and arches into me.

"Mine. You're mine," she pants.

Moving over her body, I devour her soft lips, like she is the fucking air I need to breathe. Sliding my hand between her legs, I push her panties to one side and cup her heat. My thumb rubs over her swollen clit. I push one finger in, then another. Deep inside, I stretch her tight pussy. Curling my fingers, I find her g-spot and rub, swallowing her moans down greedily as I continue devouring her lips. Feeling her body tighten, and strain for release, I slow down. Easing my lips away, I lean my forehead against hers as we try to catch our breath.

Withdrawing my fingers, I dance them up her body. When they reach her lips, I tap them there until she opens and slide them in. Her mouth engulfs both fingers, her tongue wraps around them, and she moans at her taste. The vibration of her moans ricochets through my body. The sensation of her tongue curling around, and lapping at my fingers, is almost enough to send me over the edge. I groan and bury my head into her neck.

"Fuck." I need to stop her before she has *me* begging. Yeah, who is in command now? Pulling my fingers free, I lift my head and suck her bottom lip into my mouth. I moan as her taste coats my tongue.

"Do you want me?" I breath into her mouth.

"Yes." Her whispered words hit my lips, it's all I need to know.

I kiss her again, before sliding down her body, planting soft kisses and small bites as I go. Not enough to hurt, but enough to replace the stinging sensation she craves so much from the blade of a knife, the sensation I know too well.

Not wanting to think about that right now, I drag my hands down her sides until I reach the sides of her black panties. I tug, shredding them too. Fuck, I can't wait any longer.

I bury my face in her heat, my tongue darts in and out as I lick and suck. I hold her hips firmly to the bed, forcing her to take everything my tongue is giving. *Fuck, she tastes better than I remember.* Her legs tense around my head, she's almost at her peak. I pull back, not wanting her diving over the edge too soon. She groans in protest. I do it again.

"Please, please. I need to let go," she whispers.

I don't think she realizes she has spoken, but she did. and I heard it. I heard her beg. I lap at her, press my fingers in deeply and send her head first into an orgasm that has her screaming my name. It's like music to my fucking ears. Crawling up her body, I take her lips in a deep, sensuous kiss before gazing into eyes that rock my soul and propel me into the light. Light, I haven't let myself believe was there before she came along. Pulling back, I rest my forehead against hers.

"Tell me you love me," she whispers. "I need to hear you say it again."

"I love you." I watch as a single tear rolls down her cheek before kissing it away.

"Please don't cry, it hurts to see you upset."

"Make love to me."

I kiss her and look into her eyes to see them pleading with me.

"Are you sure?" She sighs as she nods.

"Help me feel, Antonio. Please, let me know I matter."

How could I deny her anything? I would give her the whole fucking world if she asked me to.

I kiss her hard, our tongues dual. Drawing back, I climb from the bed, stand and drop my boxer briefs to the floor. Her eyes watch with want, admiration. I run my hand over my hardening length, smearing pre-cum with my fingers. I reach down to my pants and take a condom from the pocket.

"I'm clean and you know I can't..."

My eyes widen, I nod, stopping her train of thought.

"I'm clean too and I've never not worn one before." I throw the packet to the floor and crawl back up the bed, pushing her legs apart as I go. Resting one hand near her head, I run my hand down her side until I reach her knee and wrap her leg around my body. My cock brushes against her opening and I groan at the bare contact. Taking her lips in a kiss, I grab the base of my cock and slowly rub up and down through her folds before pushing inside her heat. My eyes close as her warmth wraps around me. I take a moment, open my eyes and gaze into hers. The worry is gone, the walls are down, she has let everything go. Never has she allowed anyone inside her walls, but she is letting me in. My heart does some funny shit in my chest.

"Let go, I have you now. You're safe." I rock my hips back and forth, wanting to take it slow, not wanting this moment to end.

"You promise?" She moans as her hips move with mine.

"Always. You're mine, and I'm yours." I thrust deeper, she calls out as our rhythm picks up "Fuck," I bury my face into her hair. *Fuck, she feels good.*

"Look at me," she gasps as her fingers run through my hair "I need you with me."

Lifting my head, I watch as her eyes roll back in her head. I know she is close. As I increase the speed and rock my hips, I pull her leg tighter around me.

I groan as moans leave her lips. I can't get enough of how she feels wrapped around me and the burn of her nails as they dig into the hard muscles of my back.

"Let go baby, I've got you."

She throws her head back and screams my name. The muscles of her pussy contract around me, it's enough to send me over the edge with her.

While catching my breath, I reach up and remove the lace from her eyes, leaning down I kiss the tears away.

"I love you," she breaths out before taking my mouth in a deep kiss.

I wipe the remaining tears away and gaze deep into her eyes, the truth is laid bare. "Mine," I growl before taking her mouth and moving inside her again. I know I will never get enough of my woman. No-one will *ever* hurt my Kitten again.

Chapter Ten

Katherine

Dear Diary,

Today is a good day, I feel like I can breathe again for the first time in what feels like forever. But, even on my good days, I still have the same thoughts running on replay through my head, threatening to take me back to a place I dread, but know so well. Wondering, will I ever be good enough? Wondering, how long it will take for him to wake up and leave? Wondering, have I made the right decision letting Antonio back in? But, it must be the right decision, it feels right. I can't find the words to describe how it feels to have his love, to have him claim me as his. It's like a new wall is being built, but this time we are building it together, around us. When he said he has had a black hole inside his chest and I fill it, the last couple of bricks in my wall collapsed. All that was left was me, raw, real and I saw it in his eyes when he realised I had finally broken.

I'm not perfect, and there are things I wish I could take back, but I need to move past my demons. I know I will never be one hundred percent, but maybe this is the beginning I need. I wish I could take away the pain I have caused in him.

Antonio is the reason I believe I can start afresh and push forward.

He has given me a reason to believe in myself, shown me I can be better than what I have been. I know he has scars too. I feel them beneath the tattoos covering his chest and I know from experience, where there are physical scars, there are also emotional ones. I want to be strong enough to fight my own demons and help him fight his too.

He knocks my world off its axis in the most wonderful way. I want to share my life with this man, and it's the first time ever, I have let myself believe it could be possible.

I don't want to hurt anymore, I can't walk away from this man again, not that he would let me. He sees through everything I try to hide inside me, it's as if I'm transparent to him. I never believed a love like this existed. I have nowhere to hide when it comes to him, he's peeled back the surface and he sees every hidden place within. Being so vulnerable with someone is scary as shit, but maybe it's a good thing too. Maybe for me to get better, to feel accepted, wanted, loved, I need to show him every crazy thing about me. If he can deal *with all that I am, and still stick around, then maybe opening myself up is worth every bit of happiness he wants to give me.*

What is true Happiness? Is it a smile, a touch, a whisper in the dark? Or, is it having someone who knows you inside and out and still wants to stand by you? Someone who says, no matter what, you will always be theirs. Is it too much to hope for, to dream of, to be happy, and truly free from the black hole which seems to want to steal everything good in my life? So yes, it's scary as fuck. But, life is about taking risks, and Antonio is my biggest risk of all. I will take that plunge off the deep end, and hope to God he is at the bottom to catch me. In my heart, I know he will be.

To feel like I'm nothing for most of my life, and then to have Antonio walk in and make me feel like I am his whole world, it knocks the wind out of me.

I have never let myself believe, I could have a happy ending, but maybe it's possible. I have to stop fighting it, because this pain and uncertainty I feel now, is nothing compared to what I felt without him.

When I woke with him beside me this morning, it felt like we were finally one and nothing could tear us apart. The scent of his skin, the look in his eyes, the way he let me cling to him as I fell apart in his arms, giving me his strength. The promise was there in his eyes, his word was reflected, no matter what we encountered, he would be there for me.

The voices telling me to stop fighting, give up, leave this world, are still there, but I'm stronger with Antonio by my side, and when I can't fight anymore, I know he will be there to help me through.

No, I'm not magically better. Miraculously cured. I know I will deal with this for the rest of my life, but now I have someone who loves me. Someone who truly cares and will help when I break and feel the darkness pulling me under. I'm going to listen to my heart, instead of my head, and fall into Antonio. Knowing, he will hold me up when I haven't got the strength to do so myself.

I want to know what true love is.

I want to feel again.

I want to breathe.

I want his touch.

I want his kiss.

I want to be strong.

I want to see the light.

I want to be his.

I want him to be MINE!!!

I hear the creak of the bathroom door and close my diary. After placing it on my nightstand, I watch Antonio stride into my room with a towel wrapped around him, small beads of water cling to his chest. I lick my lips as the glint of his nipple piercing catches my eye. *Fuck he's sexy.*

"Kitten, stop looking at me like you want to devour me, otherwise, I will have you on your back before you have a chance to blink."

Fuck, his deep voice, the words from his sexy mouth, causes heat to pool low in my belly. I squeeze my thighs together to ease the sudden ache there.

"We have to go over to Dom's place," Antonio says.

That snaps me from my lust fuelled haze. I remember Antonio telling me what happened at Dom's place last night and I need to make sure Brooklyn is okay after shooting the bitch from the night club. I couldn't believe what Antonio had told me.

"I'll have a quick shower." I jump to my feet and hurry toward the bathroom.

"You kept them?"

I glance over my shoulder, and see Antonio standing in front of my dressing table looking at the post-it notes.

"Of course, I did. I will never part with them." I head into the bathroom and close the door. Leaning against it for a moment, I take a deep breath, close my eyes and see the words he had written to me.

Strong, Fierce, Beautiful, and my favorite, *Loved*. Every time I felt like I was being pulled under, reading those words helped more than he will ever know. Reaching over I turn on the water, stripping myself from Antonio's shirt, I step under the hot spray and let the water work its magic on my aching body.

Pulling into the driveway at Dom's place, I reach for the door handle when Antonio parks the car.

"Kitten...."

I pause with my hand on the door and look back at Antonio. I see the sparkle in his eyes before he wraps his hand around my neck, and pulls me to him. His lips claim mine in a kiss, wrapping my arms around his neck, I deepen the kiss, loving the way he tastes. Pulling back, he rests his head against mine, we're both breathless.

"I love you," he manages to gasp.

My body tingles hearing those words, I'm still trying to believe this is actually happening.

"I love you too, Stud."

He winks before releasing me, and climbing out. I watch as he rounds the front of the car and opens my door. After stepping out, I adjust my black, high waisted skirt.

"Fuck."

I hear his growl, but before I have time to respond, my back hits the side of the car. Antonio's lips are back on mine, and I moan, wanting more. He lifts my leg, wanting to rest on his hip, but considering how tight my skirt is, it won't work. Instead, I lock my ankle around the back of his knee. I push into him and feel his hardness as he rubs into my core. I moan, he groans at the contact, and fuck, do I wish we were somewhere else right now.

A throat clears to get our attention. When he steps back, I see in his eyes, he isn't happy we have been interrupted.

"What?" he snaps, not taking his eyes off me. Frustration oozes from him.

I bite my lip to stop the giggle that wants to escape.

"Mr. Grasso, we have a warrant for your arrest."

What the fuck is happening now? My head is spinning, trying to register those words. I turn to find two police officers standing behind us. I cling to Antonio and can't believe his next words.

"I don't fucking think so, cazzo. How about you, and your mate, get back in your fucking car and get off private property."

"Not happening, Mr. Grasso. This can go easy and you can come willingly, or we can cuff you, your choice. Either way, you're coming with us."

"You have to be fucking joking, I am not going anywhere with you." Antonio starts to lead me toward the house.

Then, all hell breaks loose. The police have hold of Antonio, who is refusing to let go of me, and then I hear screaming. I think it must be me because Dominic and Brooklyn come flying out of the house, well Dominic does. Brooklyn waddles, fast.

Antonio is yelling at the police, as they push him to the hood of the car. "Get your fucking hands off her, touch her again and I promise, I will make your life fucking hell before I watch it drain from your body."

Holy, fucking, shit he's pissed. I need to get these cops hands off me. I scream at the one holding me. "Don't fucking touch me, get off me." Finally, the officer lets me go, and I run toward Antonio who is cuffed and being led to the waiting police car.

What the fuck just happened? My mind is in a daze. I see Dominic heading toward me, tears pour over my cheeks, I can't breathe. Dom's arms are around me and he's yelling at the police. "Dom, don't let this happen, I need him." I'm begging between breaths. "They can't take him from me, not now. I just got him back. No, no, no, this can't be happening."

Dom releases his hold and seems to push me toward someone else. "Sergio, take Kat inside."

I glance around and see Demetri, Sergio, and a few other men I don't recognise, standing around. They're standing, watching, doing nothing, as these fuckers take my world away.

"Don't just stand there, do something," I scream at the top of my lungs. Why aren't they doing something? Why are they letting the police take my world?

"Kat, shhh babe. Dom and his men will sort this out, let me take you inside." Brooklyn's arm is around my waist, in her other hand is the walking stick she has to use. Broken, knowing I can't do a fucking thing, I wrap my arm around her waist and we make our way up the stairs and into the house.

What the fuck just happened? Is this some cruel, sick joke? Giving me a taste of happiness, then ripping it away?

I need him back.

He's MINE!!!

Chapter Eleven

Antonio

I look around the sterile interview room, with its clinical white walls and sparse furniture, and note the tape recorder set up on the small table in front of me. I sit, lean back in my chair and let out a frustrated sigh. This isn't the first time I have been in one of these rooms, and if truth be told, it won't be the last. I close my eyes and try not to focus on the piece of shit cop who had his hands all over my woman. I can still hear her screams, it makes my blood boil. Sure, I could have taken them both out, but doing that would have led to more shit. So, I let them cuff me. Taking another look around, I note a camera in the corner near the ceiling. A red light blinks on and off. Fuckers. I turn my attention toward the door when it opens, and see the two fuckers who cuffed me enter the room. I stare down the piece off shit who manhandled my girl. I smirk when he looks away. Fucking pussy.

"Mr Grasso, do you know why you are here?" The cazzo who cuffed me slides a folder across the table. I don't answer, I'm telling them nothing. I'm no fucking rat, and I don't like cops.

Shaking his head when I don't say anything, he sits in front of me and opens the folder.

The piece of shit, who touched my woman takes the other seat in front of me. "It would be in your best interest if you confess now, and would save wasting anymore time."

I lean forward and rest my hands on the table, take a quick look down at the opened folder and notice a bruised and bloody face. What the fuck? I keep my emotions and expression in check, and focus on the dickhead who cuffed me. I still don't say a word.

"Okay, let's play it your way then," Dickhead one says. "You're under arrest for the assault on one Ashley Jane Alexander, stand up and place your hands behind your back."

I stand without arguing, and keep my mouth shut, but all the while my thoughts are going a hundred miles an hour. Who the fuck is Ashley Jane Alexander?

The realization hits me hard, Kitten's fucking sister. Fuck. They cuff me and lead me from the room, but I know Dom and my lawyer will be here soon.

I hope to fuck Katherine is okay and she's still with Brooklyn. When she hears what the fuck is going on, I know she is going to blame herself. The black cloud which hangs over her, is going to try and suck her back into its clutches, and I won't be there to fucking stop it. Brooklyn needs to make sure my woman is okay.

Dickhead two speaks low so only I hear, "your girl felt good in my arms. She's got some fight in her, that one. Hmm, love me a feisty girl in bed."

I stop dead in my tracks before he can say another word, I snap the cuffs in half and pin him to the wall by the throat. I speak calmly, deathly low, so only he can hear, and let him know, he just signed his death warrant. "You go anywhere near my girl again, so much as breath on her, and I will have you begging me to end your life." I cluck my tongue. "No, sorry. Too late. You're going to pay with your life, remember that the next time you close your eyes, fucker."

I'm pulled from the asshole, and take great pleasure in watching him drop to the floor, holding his neck, gasping for breath.

Katherine

It's been ten days since I've been allowed to see Antonio, and every day I think about the blade. I crave the stinging sensation, but resist the dark thoughts. I need to be strong, and not succumb to the darkness trying to pull me under. I need to prove to Antonio, I have this shit sorted, and under control.

The first night was the hardest, going home to an empty house. Walking into my bedroom, laying on the bed where his scent lingered. I had to summon every ounce of strength I had, to not walk into the bathroom and end it all right then. I fought to prevent the darkness from consuming me. Fighting the urges, I grabbed my diary, and reread what I had written a few hours before.

After reading, instead of doing what I normally would, allowing the darkness to win, I packed a bag and headed back to Brooklyn and Dominic's. I knew I wouldn't be able to survive this without their help, so I have been staying with them.

So, ten days later I'm walking into the visitor's area of the prison to visit my man. I can't believe the lengths I had to go to, the hoops I had to jump through, to get in here. My bag was taken away and X-rayed while I walked through a metal detector, I was then subjected to an eye scan. Having Sergio, my new bodyguard, and Dominic with me, didn't help make things easier. But, I wouldn't have changed anything, and I needed them here with me for support.

No-one has told me why Antonio is still here, and he refuses to talk to me on the phone. He told Dominic, he wants to speak to me in person. God, I hope that's true. I am terrified he's not speaking to me because he's had second thoughts and doesn't want me.

I glance around and notice other inmates sitting with their visitors at round metal tables with matching stools, both are attached to the floor.

Dom places his hand on my shoulder, I take a deep breath and let it out slowly. Moments later, Antonio appears from a side door, he's dressed in a white jumpsuit, hands cuffed at the front, guards by his side. His head is lowered, eyes on the floor. I know the moment he senses I'm here, his head snaps up and his eyes lock on mine. My heart squeezes in my chest with the look of longing and fierce possession he is directing at me. A surreal energy surrounds us, time stops, no-one else is here, no noise. The connection is broken when a guard steps in front of him, blocking him from view. Blocking him from approaching.

I turn toward Dom, confused. I silently beg the powers that be, not to take him away before we can speak.

Dom steps closer and whispers, "you have to be seated before the guards will allow the visit." He nods to indicate a table in the far corner and I hurry toward it.

Sergio holds out a chair, I sit and brush the tears from my cheeks. I need him to see I'm doing okay, he needs to know I'm staying strong. For us.

Dom and Sergio take a seat beside me leaving a stool between me and Sergio. I gaze at Antonio as he approaches. When he reaches us, he leans over, grabs the back of my neck and slams his mouth down on mine. I'm in absolute shock, and freeze, because I was warned, we are not allowed to touch each other. Fuck 'em. After a moment I relax and let his taste consume me. Fuck, I have missed him more than I ever thought possible.

I lift my hands and rake my nails down the side of his face, I feel the shiver which causes his body to tremble.

I hear shouting in the distance, but I don't take any notice. Every thought, every worry, every bit of love I possess, pours from me into that one kiss. Easing back, he rests his forehead against mine. I caress his face with my fingertips, the tingle of warmth spreads through me and I gaze into his eyes.

"Kitten, fuck, I have missed you, baby."

"I've missed you too, so much. I need you to come home."

He sits next to me, grasps my hand and squeezes. I relax into his side, loving the feeling of being near him again.

Antonio shakes hands with Dom and then Sergio.

"Brother," Dom says. "You almost caused a fucking riot in here with that show."

"Fuck 'em. They'll get over it. Everyone here knows who I am, and now they know not to lay eyes on my woman"

"Si," Dom nods, chuckling.

I lean my head on his shoulder, close my eyes and breath him in. They are speaking in Italian, I don't bother listening. Instead, I bask in the vibration of his deep voice as it moves through my cheek, and wraps around my heart. Every so often, I feel his lips press against my forehead in a soft kiss, and when I sigh, he squeezes my hand. For the first time since he was arrested, I feel content, relaxed, safe.

"Kitten," Antonio nudges me.

"Mmmm."

"Kitten, wake up."

I snap my eyes open, fuck I must have dozed off. I haven't slept much with Antonio not by my side.

"I'm sorry." I wipe my hand across my mouth just in case I have drooled all over the place.

I feel Antonio's lips on my forehead again. "Did you hear what I said?"

I shake my head, I have no fucking idea.

"I will be home sometime next week. My lawyer was finally able to set a court date to arrange bail. When I'm home, we'll talk about everything then, si?"

When I sit back, I look into his eyes see the worry as he subconsciously rubs the scars on my wrist. I need to reassure him, I'm okay.

"I'm fine, I promise. Please, don't worry about me. I'm staying with Brooklyn and Dominic, and if I need to go out anywhere, Sergio is with me."

He growls with displeasure, his eyes narrow. He's not happy about Sergio being with me, but there is nothing he can do about it right now.

I lean forward and plant a kiss on his lips. "I'm fine, do what you need to, so we can be together." I feel some of the tension leave his body.

"I love you, Kitten, so fucking much."

"I love you too, Stud and I'll be there when you come home."

He shakes Dom and Sergio's hands again, says something in Italian, leans into me, kisses me gently before whispering into my ear, "when you're struggling, close your eyes and feel me inside your heart. I will *always* be there."

I close my eyes as his lips graze mine again. I let his words burrow deep inside me.

When I open my eyes, he's gone and my tears begin flowing. *I can do this. I have to be fine. Just a couple more days and we'll be together again.*

The words play on a loop, as once again, I am forced to walk away and leave my world behind.

Chapter Twelve

Katherine

Dear Diary,

I know it's been eleven days since I last wrote to you, but how can you write about something when you have no clue how to put it into words? Antonio was ripped away from me eleven days ago, and I feel like I'm in a constant haze. The pain is worse this time because I had no say in the matter, and I couldn't stop what was happening. Yes, I have felt the black hole calling my name, and trying to drag me down, but I'm doing everything I can to not let it take control. Antonio needs me to be strong right now, I know he must be going crazy not being able to be with me. When he kissed me yesterday, I felt everything he is feeling - the longing, the anger. It tore my heart apart to walk away and leave him there, but what choice did I have? What did I ever do to deserve so much hurt?

I'm not sure what's worse, him being taken away, or the fact no one will tell me what the fuck is going on. I tried to talk to Dominic about it yesterday on our way home, but he wouldn't say a word. He insists, Antonio doesn't want me to worry, and will tell me when he comes home.

I had to give a statement to Alfio, the family lawyer. It was to verify Antonio's whereabouts the morning before the police turned up. When I asked Alfio what was going on, he simply told me, he wasn't at liberty to discuss the issue. He then looked at Dom over my shoulder.

Something bad has happened, or is happening, why the fuck won't anyone talk to me? I know it's bad, otherwise Antonio would be with me now. I'm done, I can't sit around and wait for someone to answer my questions, I need to do some investigating myself. I need my man home with me – now!

I'll think of a way to get what I need and give Sergio the slip at the same time.

Closing my diary, I push it to one side, lie on the bed, and stare through the floor to ceiling windows lining the wall next to me. I watch the water and ships in the distance while trying to think of where to start on my investigations. Maybe when I go to the cafe in the morning, I can slip out the back door without Sergio seeing me. Or, I can go to Gwen's and ask her for help. I let out an exasperated sigh, where the fuck do I start? Throwing my arm across my face, I groan loudly.

"Aunty Kat." Evie says from my open door.

"Hey babydoll, what are you doing?"

Shrugging her shoulders, she makes her way over to me and crawls next to me on the bed. "Do you miss uncle Antonio?"

"Yeah Babydoll, I miss him a lot."

"You know you can always hug me, when you miss him, and Daddy said he'll be home soon."

"I know." I hug her closer and stare through the windows, we stay like that until Evie pulls back and smiles at me.

"Mommy and me are going shopping to buy stuff to make daddy dinner, do you want to come?"

Her bright blue eyes light up and she bats those damn eyelashes at me. How can I tell her no when she does that?

"Okay, what is mom cooking?" Grabbing my hand, she pulls me upright. As much as I want to lay in bed all day, maybe a little shopping trip with my girls would help.

"Not sure, we should ask."

We head down the stairs and I come to an abrupt stop when I hear Dominic yelling in his office. I don't understand what he's saying, because he's speaking Italian.

"Alfio, I don't give a fuck what that stupid bitch has said, I want Antonio home and the bitch dealt with."

There's a pause before he speaks again. I stay still, listening. "I don't care what you have to do, Demetri will be at your office at noon, get it done."

I feel sick, my stomach is churning, what the fuck is Dom talking about?

"Aunty Kat come on," Evie tugs on my hand and draws my attention to her. I shake off thoughts of the conversation for now, and head into the living room. I find Brooklyn on the sofa surrounded by wedding magazines, the television is on the music channel.

"Hey Dollface, what are you doing?" I look around at the mess she has made while Evie lays on the floor.

"Dominic had these delivered this morning, and told me to relax, and choose whatever I wanted."

"Why do you have a strange look on your face, something wrong?"

"I'm fine. There is a lot to consider, and I never in my life thought I could have any of this." She waves her hand over the mess of magazines before continuing. "It's a little overwhelming, I guess."

Pushing some magazines aside, I sit beside my friend. She hands me one which is open showing pictures of pretty flowers, dresses and cakes.

"I'm pretty sure whatever you pick will be fine, honey."

"Yeah, I know. I just want to be beautiful for Dom."

"You will be." I change the subject because she looks like she needs to take a breather. Evie said you were going shopping?"

"Yeah, I'm going to cook a special dinner tonight. Dom's been stressed lately, and I don't want him having to worry about it."

I had noticed Dom cooks almost every night. "How about we clean this up, and get ready. I'll let Sergio know what our plans are."

"Sounds good." Brooklyn pushes up on her walking stick and bends over to pick up the magazines. I stop her with my hand on her shoulder just as Dom walks into the room.

"Angel, I have to head out for a bit."

I study Dom when he speaks and notice how tired he appears.

"Okay, Big Man." Brooklyn slowly makes her way over to him. When she is close, he wraps his arms around her waist, pulls her into his chest and whispers something in her ear which makes her giggle.

I glance at Evie, she is sitting on the floor colouring in, but takes a moment to look toward them and rolls her eyes with a smile on her face. I bite my lip to stop myself laughing at the look on her face.

"Come on Babydoll, let's go and get ready." I extend my hand and wait for her to pack up her crayons before we leave the room. I think it's perfect timing when I hear Dom growl something in Brooklyn's ear.

Strolling the aisles of the supermarket, I ponder the snippet of conversation I heard from Dom's office earlier.

"Earth to Katherine," Brooklyn nudges me with her shoulder. "What has you off with the pixies?"

I glance toward Evie, she's occupied looking at the flavoured ice-cream in the glass freezer. I turn back to Brooklyn, wondering if she knows what's going on, but isn't telling me. I'm not sure if it would upset me if she knows, and refuses to tell me.

"Do you know why Antonio was arrested?"

"No, Dom won't tell me."

"So, you asked him?"

"Of course, I did, but he knows if he tells me, I would tell you."

"Would you?"

"Of course, I would, you're my sister. I would tell you in a heartbeat."

I blow out the breath, I didn't realize I was holding. I'm relieved to know she would tell me. I nod and smile.

"Come on, I need to grab the sauce for dinner, then we can leave. My leg is starting to hurt."

I feel bad that she is in pain, and there's nothing I can do to stop it. I call Evie over, grab her hand and we head to the sauce aisle.

"Aunty Kat, can we buy popcorn so we can watch movies tonight?"

"We don't need popcorn to watch movies, Babydoll." I laugh at the pout on her face and look at Brooklyn when I hear her laughing. I roll my eyes before looking back at Evie. When I notice her hands together like she is praying, I burst into laughter.

"Please," she begs, batting those long eyelashes of hers.

Why the hell did I teach her that move? I look back at Brooklyn, and notice the, *this is your own fault,* look on her face. Yeah, big help my best friend turned out to be.

"Will you be okay if we hurry and grab some popcorn?" I speak a little too sweetly causing Brooklyn to crack up laughing.

"Yeah, I'm fine. Go get the girl what she wants, you always do." She laughs again and turns back to the shelves in front of her.

"Babydoll, you're supposed to use that look on your mother, not me," I say as we walk away.

"I do, oh and on daddy too, he can never say no to me." She belly laughs before going on, "and now it works on you too."

I open my mouth to say something smart when I hear Brooklyn scream.

"Noooo, no, no!"

Evie looks at me, terrified. I grab her hand and we rush back to where we left her mother. "What's wrong? What happened?" I pat Brooklyn down from head to toe, wondering what the fuck happened. Tears stream down her face. I grasp her shoulders. "What happened, Brooklyn. Talk to me." I'm panicking now, she won't answer me, she keeps sobbing. I reach into my pocket, pull out my phone, and call Dominic. Placing it to my ear, I listen to it ring. I'm still trying to work out what the fuck happened.

"Brooklyn, are you hurt? Tell me what happened, Dollface, please"

"Kat what's wrong?" I hear the alarm in Dom's voice.

"I don't know. I heard her scream when Evie and I went to get popcorn and now she's crying full on. She won't tell me what's wrong."

"Brooklyn talk to me," I try again.

Clearing her eyes of the tears, and catching her breath, she points to the shelves filled with sauces.

"Kat, what the fuck is happening, what's wrong with Brooklyn?" Dom yells in my ear. "Where's Evie?"

"Standing with us."

"Where the fuck are you? And where the fuck is Sergio?"

I tell him where we are, explain Sergio is waiting near the car, and hang up.

"Brooklyn, Dom's on the way. Can you please tell me what the fuck just happened?"

Appearing to calm, she looks at me seriously. The next thing out of her mouth has me trying not to lose my mind, laughing. What in the actual fuck!

"They don't have the sauce I want."

"What?"

"The sauce I wanted for dinner tonight, they don't have any left."

"Are you seriously telling me, you lost your shit because they sold out of the sauce you wanted?" I bite my lip, because this has to be the most fucked up thing I have ever dealt with. "Are you telling me, I just rang your mob boss fiancé, over a bottle of sauce?"

"It's a really yummy sauce," she sobs.

That does it, Evie and I exchange a look, before bursting into laughter.

"Brooklyn..." She's sobbing hard again and I try to soothe her. Then, I hear people running toward us, and Dom's voice calls out.

"Angel, what happened, are you hurt?"

"I'm fine now." She moves into his arms.

"What the fuck happened?" He glares at everyone looking on.

"They ran out of the sauce I wanted to use for dinner tonight." Brooklyn explains like it's the end of the world.

"Angel, what are you on about?"

"I wanted to cook dinner tonight, you've been so stressed and I wanted to do something special for you. But, now I can't because they haven't got the sauce I need." She sniffs back the tears, and I try and look somewhere else, because this is insane.

"Si, I get that, but why are you crying?"

"I don't know, I just really wanted that sauce."

I am trying not to laugh, but it's hard when I look at Dom, and he's biting his lip to stop himself from laughing as he pulls Brooklyn into his chest.

"Um, I think maybe her hormones are a bit out of whack. I'm sorry I called, but I thought she was hurt, *physically*." I use air quotes when I say physically, because I do believe Brooklyn has finally lost her damn mind. Whoa!!! Dom chuckles and when I swing around, I notice Sergio is doing his best not to laugh.

"Si, okay. Angel how about I take you girls home, and we'll order something in. Tell Sergio what sauce you need, and he can go and find it. You can cook your special dinner tomorrow night."

Brooklyn nods and starts walking off with Dom.

Evie grabs my hand, and we follow behind them. I look down at Evie and know she is confused every bit as much as me. My fucking head is spinning with what just happened.

"Aunty Kat, are my brothers already causing mommy to go crazy?"

"Yeah, I believe so, Babydoll."

We both crack up laughing.

Dom turns toward us and winks; obviously, he's heard what we are talking about.

Chapter Thirteen

Antonio

Kat was so fucking sexy in her tight, body hugging black jeans and black singlet shirt when she visited yesterday. Having her lips on mine, our tongues devouring each other's mouths, was enough to settle the beast inside me. But, only for a short time. It took everything in me, not to strip her bare, and take her right there on the table. Then, I would have had to kill everyone who had seen my woman naked, or heard her moans of pleasure. I didn't miss the looks on the other inmates faces when she came in, leering at my woman like animals. I wanted to kill every fucking one of them for daring to even glance her way. Having her in my arms, feeling her curves pushing into my side, eventually calmed me.

I refuse to tell Kat, and have warned Dom, that no-one is to say a word about her sister being the reason I'm in here, until I can be with her. I don't know what the fuck she would do if she knew, but I can guess she would explode with anger, and go after Ashley. Then, she would shatter into a thousand pieces. I need to keep my woman safe, and be there to help her get through it, when she finds out.

I know she has Brooklyn, but I want to be the one to tell her, to pick up the pieces. Maybe that's fucking selfish, but I don't give a fuck. It's *my* job to take care of her now, and I'll be damned if I let anyone get in my way - Boss's woman, or not. Kitten is MINE.

Laying back on the thin foam mattress, I feel the metal springs digging into my back. I raise my hands and tuck them under my head, close my eyes, and imagine being in bed with Kat snuggled up beside me. I snap out of my day dream when I hear the rattle of keys, the guards are unlocking the cell doors. I stand and stretch, trying to get rid of the kinks and knots in my back. Reaching over toward the television, which sits on box shelves attached to the grubby green/blue walls, I flip the switch to off. After carefully folding the letter I was writing to my Kitten, I push it under my pillow. I glance around the small cell, it feels like it was made for a fucken Leprechaun. Do they usually only jail fucking midgets? There are two metal beds, one attached to each wall, a small as fuck shower, wash basin and toilet. I peer out through the window in the center of the wall above the beds, thick bars distort the view over the rear yard. I'm glad I don't have someone else in here with me, it's to fucken small with only me in it.

"Grasso, step back," one of the guards calls out. I see his eyes as he looks through the small window in the door. Following his order, I don't want to be here any longer than necessary, I take a step back and wait to hear the click of the lock. The door is left ajar, and I watch as they move away before stepping through and heading toward the small common area. I find a couple of other guys setting up to play cards.

Taking a seat at a metal table, I scan my surroundings. It's something I always do when I first come out of my cell. Everyone here knows exactly who I am, and even though they are scared shitless of me, there are still some pieces of shit who think they have the balls to take me on. I take note of other inmates coming down the stairs from the cells on the floor above. A few head toward the other end of the block where a door leads outside to the yard where there is an exercise section and another seating area. I notice a Chinese guy side eye me as he heads to the wash area behind the staircase. I don't break eye contact with him until he looks away. I know exactly who he is, he's a member of the ghost dragons gang in Sydney. That fucker Joey beat up one of their women.

"Grasso, you in?"

"Si, I'll be back." I stand and stride toward the wash area, walk up behind the cazzo and wait for him to turn around and notice me.

"You got a problem?" I growl out. When he starts jabbering in Chinese, saying God only knows what, I fold my arms across my chest and demand, "English, motherfucker."

"Your boss better watch his back." He smirks as if he knows some secret joke I'm not in on. When he turns away, I grab the fucker by his shirt, and pull him up onto his toes. He tries to wrestle free from my hold but it isn't happening. "Is that a threat?" I spit out.

"Grasso," a guard yells, and I drop the piece of shit on the concrete floor, he gasps for air. "La tua morte,"(you're dead) I growl out before turning, and walking back to the table. I could have taken him right there and then, I have some privileges in here being who I am, but I don't want to push too much and end up having to do more time away from my girl.

"Everything good, Antonio?" Pete, another inmate asks as I return to the table and sit.

He's a decent guy, I guess, if you can call a murderer a decent person. I can't judge considering what I do for a living.

Taking my silence to be his answer, he deals the cards and I replay the threat from that piece of shit Chinese.

"So, your girl came to visit you yesterday?"

I'm pulled from my thoughts when I hear Pete ask about Kat, why the fuck is he bringing her up?

"What's your point?" I ask, already on edge from the other fucker. My anger is starting to get the better of me. I'm in no mood for him to be speaking about my woman.

Pete obviously senses my foul mood. "Easy mate, we're just shooting the breeze."

Fucker. "Let's just fucking play." I glare at him. daring him to say another word. I then turn my glare on the other two fuckers at the table. They are quick to realize, I'm not in the fucking mood for this shit, and look back down at their cards.

Fuck, I need air. Throwing the cards onto the table, I get to my feet and head for the yard. But, I know that ain't going to calm me down, I need to get the fuck out of here, and hold my girl in my arms.

Chapter Fourteen

Katherine

Dear Diary,

Today is the day I'm determined to get some answers, because I need to fight for what I want. I have been fighting my whole life to stop the hurt, to stop the demons, and now I need to fight a little harder. I won't lose him.

I tossed and turned all night wondering what the hell to do, trying to figure out what the hell I want. The answer? I want it all! I want to be so much in love, it hurts. I want the kind of love that makes my skin prickle when I think about him, when he's near. I want mind-blowing sex that has me begging for more. I want that special connection with my one true soul mate, the one you can't live without. A person who is your one true safe place. A person who, no matter what happens, bad or good, they are there to hold you; to pull you close so the connection is so strong, no-one could ever break it. I want someone who makes me feel sexy, smart, silly, serious, sinful and satisfied. I want someone to make me laugh until my drink spurts from my nose. I want to finish someone's sentence, but most of all, I want to believe in someone, in something, in a future I never knew I could ever have. That someone, that special person, my true soul mate, is Antonio and I will get him back.

So, yes, I'm going to take a risk today. I'll face down my demons, and get the man I want above all others, back home to me so we can finally have our happy ending. I'm tired of hiding behind a wall, a wall I thought was my protection but in fact, was my downfall.

I thought hard about it all last night and I think I have connected the dots. Dom's conversation, and the fact Antonio doesn't want me knowing anything until he is home, convinces me, they are talking about my bitch of a sister. She has something to do with my man being in jail. I think they may be worried about how I might react, or fear the black hole may swallow me whole.

But, I'm not feeling like crawling under the covers, and crying about some betrayal, no, just the opposite, I'm ready to kick her fucking ass.

Antonio is my soul mate, the man who has me feeling like I can breathe again. If my asshole sister thinks she can take him from me, if she thinks she can break me, she needs to fucking think again.

No! She hasn't broken me, she has pushed me to get stronger. For the first time in my life, she can get fucked because, this time, I'm taking back what's MINE!

Closing my diary, I place it on the nightstand and push up from the bed. The time on the small clock reads 4.30am. I grab my jumper from the end of the bed and creep to the door. I try not to make a sound so as not to wake everyone up. Easing the door slightly open, I peek out into the hall way. A single lamp casts a dim light, enough to see where you're going without running into things. It's mainly left on for Evie in case she wakes during the night and is scared. I quickly scan the area, no-one is around and I don't hear a sound. I open the door, slip through, and quickly, and quietly, make my way toward the stairs.

The front door is locked, but the key is left in. After hurrying through, I close the door behind me and look around to make sure none of Dom's men are around. It's still dark, but barely. I need to leave before the sun starts to rise and I'm seen. I can't take my car so on foot it is. I slink between the bushes of the long driveway so as not to be seen. I know Sergio is on guard somewhere, and I can't risk him seeing me. He would either follow me, or more likely take me back inside to Dom. I can't let that happen, I need to take care of this myself, and I can't allow anyone to stop me.

I'm not sure how I managed it without being seen, but I'm home. Fuck my feet are killing me from walking so far. I'm glad a taxi came by when I was halfway home, otherwise it would have taken me a hell of a lot longer than it did.

Running up the stairs, I head into my room and search my nightstand for the small handgun Antonio left there when he first heard about Darren. Finding it, I slip it into the back pocket of my jeans. I reach under the bed and grab my backpack before hurrying back downstairs. I throw a water bottle, phone, keys and wallet inside the backpack then head for the door. I'm ready to get this shit done, finished. I have a good idea where I'm heading. The last time Ashley got into trouble, and needed money, I had to go pay her drug dealer. I guess I'll start there, but first I need to make a quick stop.

Walking up the small path to the front door, I raise my hand to knock and take a deep breath. I hope I'm not dragging them out of bed, it's only 6.30 in the morning. I knock and wait, but don't hear anything on the other side of the door. I raise my arm to knock one last time, when the door opens, and Harry is standing there with a smile on his face.

"Sweetheart, what brings you here this early in the morning?" He leans over and wraps his arms around me in a warm hug. I melt a little in his arms, grateful he isn't upset with me for calling so early.

"Morning Harry, I hope I didn't wake you."

"Not at all. Gwen was putting the kettle on, and I was coming to grab the newspaper, when I heard the knock on the door."

137

"May I come in?"

"Of course, head into the kitchen, Gwen should be there."

"Thanks, Harry." I nod, head down the small hall, and into the kitchen where I find Gwen making coffee.

Gwen smiles when she sees me. "Morning, sweetheart, take a seat and I'll makes us a cuppa then we can talk."

I sit at the bench. "How did you know I wanted to talk?"

Gwen picks up the kettle when it boils and pours hot water into three coffee cups. "Katherine, I have known you for a long time, and I know the last time you were here this early, was just before you brought Brooklyn and Evie home to us. I may be old, but I'm not silly." She chuckles and smiles at me.

"I'm sorry." I bow my head, feeling guilty.

"Now stop that, you have nothing to be sorry about. Tell me what's going on?" She places a coffee cup in front of me.

Wrapping my hands around the hot cup, I take a small sip before speaking. "Ashley had Antonio arrested. I'm not sure what the charges are, and I don't care. He didn't do anything to her." My words tumble out, and I hope she believes me. She stays quiet for a moment, and I'm worried she may believe he actually did something to her.

"Your sister was always trouble, Kat. Her causing trouble for Antonio is not news to us, and we know she plays head games with you. Now, before you get your back up, and ask why I didn't tell you we have known all along, hear me out. You built a wall around yourself a long time ago, but back then, there was no way I could say something that may make you shrink inside yourself any further. I told her to stay away from you, that I knew about her drug issues, and if she caused any more trouble for you, I would go to the police. She seemed to take the hint, but your mum fell ill, then Nancy, your Grandmother. It was a lot for you to take on, and every day, Harry and I saw you withdraw a little more. When you brought the cafe with the money your grandmother left you, I loved being there every day with you, helping get it off the ground, and watching you smile for the first time in a long time. You were finally finding yourself again. When Brooklyn came back, I thought you helping her, may help you too."

She pauses and smiles before continuing. "Seeing you with Antonio, made us so happy, we knew he would be the one to help you mend. He didn't take your shit, and you sure as hell didn't take his." She laughs before speaking again. "I saw how he affected you, and how you struggled to let him. He brought out the fire we know lives within you and he handled the storm of emotions you try so hard to hide. It took you a while, and we know you struggled with wanting to let him in. But, Katherine, no-one could tell you what to do, you had to work it out for yourself, you had to make the decision on whether you wanted to let him in or walk away. I'm so pleased you fought for him. I know I've gone off track here, sorry about that, but I needed you to know; you think you hide your feelings from the world, but the people closest to you, who love you unconditionally, see your struggles without you having to say a word."

Taking a sip of her coffee, she leans against the stove.

I sniff a little, and wipe the tears which have fallen.

"I love him, I won't let that bitch take him away from me. She has tried to destroy me too many times over the years. Every time she is finished with me, I struggle to pick up the pieces, but this time, I'm not going to let it happen. She is not winning this time. I need to fight her, Gwen, with everything I have. Without Antonio, I don't think I could pull myself away from that dark hole I circle every day."

Reaching over, she places her warm hand on mine, and I remember her arms being around me while I fell apart; when mom died, then grandma, and when I thought I had failed Brooklyn. Being here, and talking with Gwen, helps me to believe the things which happened in the past, weren't my fault.

"The decision you make next, will be the right one." Harry speaks from where he is leaning against the doorway.

I look over, and I see the acceptance in his eyes. When I turn back to Gwen, I notice she is nodding and smiling. I feel a little lighter knowing, no matter what I choose to do next, they are with me all the way. I'm not sure why I felt the need to come here, but I'm glad I did. What I have decided to do next, could end up in one of two ways. Me, living my happy ending with the man of my dreams. Or Me, not coming back at all and finally letting the darkness completely consume me.

Chapter Fifteen

Antonio

"Grasso, you have a phone call." I look toward the guard who called out to me, do another push-up and get to my feet. I grab my shirt from the table, wipe the sweat from my face and chest, and head toward the guard. Inmates aren't usually allowed phone calls, but being who I am has its perks. One of the guards owes Dominic a favour, so that helps too.

Heading through the common area, I follow the guard into the office and nod my greeting to another guard who is seated. He stands, I take his seat and grab the phone.

"Capo," I say in greeting.

"Brother." The Boss' voice sounds strained and I immediately go on alert.

"What's happened?"

"It's Katherine." He pauses and the hairs on the back of my neck stand on end. "She's missing."

My temper goes from zero to exploding in a millisecond. "What the fuck do you mean, she's missing. Where the fuck is she?" I take deep breaths in an attempt to control my anger, but it isn't working.

Dom starts to explain. "Somehow, she managed to slip out unnoticed, probably in the early hours of this morning. We thought she was exhausted and sleeping in, but when Brooklyn went to wake her about 11 am, she was gone. I have all the boys out searching, but so far they're coming up empty. It's like she's vanished into thin air."

I glance the clock on the wall, it's almost 5pm. Where the fuck would she be? I rack my brain for anything right now, but I'm coming up blank.

"Did you check with Gwen?" I have to ask but I know it would have been the first place they would have checked.

"Si, Gwen said she was there early this morning. Kat said she was going to sort some things out with her sister, and she'd be home by lunchtime."

Her sister, why the fuck would she go in search of her? Then it hits me - she knows! She fucking knows!!

"Dom, she knows about the charges, how the fuck did she find out?"

"Fuck, I don't know. I didn't tell her, or Brooklyn. My woman is losing her shit and I'm trying to calm her ass the fuck down. I have Alfio sorting your papers, so we can get you released as soon as possible."

"When?" I snap, knowing I need to get out of here. Fuck. I need to find my girl before she does something stupid or gets hurt.

"Papers will be submitted for urgent response first thing tomorrow. You should be out by the afternoon, or early the next day"

"Fuck, it's too long. I need to get out now."

"Antonio, we *will* find her. Sergio is running down where her sister is."

"Sergio was supposed to watch her to begin with, where the fuck was he?"

"Look other shit has happened while you have been inside and he can't be everywhere at once. I haven't got time to explain right now so, get your shit together and be ready to kiss that fucking place goodbye."

He disconnects the call, and I slam the phone down, pissed that this shit has happened. I feel like a fucking caged animal right now. I get that Dom's pissed, and I shouldn't have jumped down his throat, but fuck, my girl is missing. She could be fucking hurt, or worse, fucking dead. I have to calm my fucking ass down. Fuck, I need to get the fuck out of here.

Two days later

Antonio

After nearly two weeks of hell, I finally get to walk out of this shit hole. But, I don't get to walk out into the arms of my girl. No, instead, the first person I see is Sergio standing next to a black *Lexus* SUV. I hurriedly cross the carpark, I'm anxious to get home and find out where the fuck my girl is. Dominic rang again last night to let me know she is still missing, the papers for my release had been approved, and Sergio would be here to bring me home. It's been the longest three fucking days of my life knowing Kat's missing, and not fucking knowing anything is driving me fucking crazy.

"Capo Bastone," Sergio greets me.

"Si, brother, it's good to see you." I shake his hand before getting into the front seat of the car. I'm still pissed he let Kat get away from him, but if I know my girl, which I do, nothing would have stopped her.

"So, do we know anything new?"

"Boss rang while I was waiting for you to come out, he said we may have a lead at an old warehouse not far from here."

"In Sydney?" What the fuck? Why would there be a lead here?

He nods and I know he is thinking the same as me. "I don't fucking know Capo Bastone, but we are going to find out. There's a present for you in the glovebox."

Leaning forward in my seat, I pop it open and see my Colt Super 38's. Taking them out, I weigh them in my hands before slipping them into the back waistband of my jeans.

144

"Well let's get this shit over and done with. I want my woman back, and God help the figlia di madre (motherfucker) who has her. They are going to wish they had never been born once I'm finished with them."

Sergio starts the car, and we fall silent as he weaves through the traffic on the way to the warehouse. I'm trying to work out why she would be in Sydney, nothing is making sense.

"Sergio, where is your phone?"

Pulling the phone from his jacket pocket, he passes it to me.

"Who are you calling?"

"Theo. Things aren't adding up, it feels like we're missing something."

"Si," Sergio nods.

Dialing the phone, I place it to my ear and listen as it rings.

"Si, Sergio," Theo answers.

"It's me, why the fuck is there a lead in Sydney?"

"Capo bastone, Kat's credit card was used at a garage to buy fuel. I had been monitoring her phone, but it had been switched off. When she stopped to use her credit card, I hoped she might have turned her phone on. The tracer you had installed, flashed up on my screen. It was moving before it finally stopped at an old warehouse on the outskirts of the city."

The more he talks, the more I feel my anger growing and getting the better of me. "Let me know if the signal moves."

145

"Si, Capo Bastone."

I disconnect the call. "Sergio, we need to get there now. Fuck, the tracker on her phone is on and if it moves, Theo will let us know."

Sergio eases his foot down on the accelerator and I feel the car increase speed. I grip the phone in my hand, praying we aren't too late.

Sergio pulls the car to a stop at the kerb across the street from an old run down warehouse. A white van is parked on the other side, it doesn't look like it's been used in a long time. I'm on edge and feel the blood hammering in my veins. I can't just sit here.

"What do you think, Capo Bastone?" Sergio asks.

"I don't know, but we are wasting time sitting out here. Let's make a move."

Nodding his agreement, we climb from the car and make our way over to the side of the warehouse where the van is parked. I pull one of the guns from my waistband as I squint to look through a filthy car window. The vehicle is empty, except for a backpack sitting on the passenger seat. I signal Sergio and nod toward the old rusted door on the side of the warehouse.

A high-pitched scream breaks through the silence, and echoes in my ears. *Fuck, my girl!* Gun raised, I kick through the door. I can't see a fucking thing through the darkness, the only light, two slivers from the dirty windows overhead, reveals nothing. *Fuck, where is she?* Adrenaline pumps through my body, I look toward Sergio, he's aiming his gun and searching as frantically as me. Signaling to him, I bring a finger to my lips so I can hear where the hell she is. I hear a slight whimper, then a man's voice coming from the left, at the back of the building.

We hurry in the direction of the whimpers and I note the light illuminating the bottom of the door. Without wasting any time, I bring my foot back and kick in the door. I raise my gun, ready to shoot at the guy standing over my girl who is cowered in the corner. His hand is raised and he's holding a belt ready to hit her. He turns at the sound of the door crashing open, and I get a good look at his face. It's fucking Joey, the piece of shit.

My attention is drawn to a small fire in a fireplace in the corner, and an old desk and chair with dirt and dust covering everything. I bring my attention back to the cazzo in front of me, he looks like he hasn't bathed in weeks. He's dressed in dirty clothes and unshaven.

"Sergio, get Kat out of here while I tie up this figlia di madre. The Boss has been looking for you, Joey, he has special plans for you." It's taking everything in me not to pull the trigger, but I know the boss wants him alive.

His eyes dart around the room nervously, he's searching for a way out, but there's none. And, he would have to get through me first. That's not going to fucking happen. I watch Sergio crouch down, and start talking to my girl. It takes her a moment, but she finally allows him to pick her up.

"Antonio," Joey says, bringing my attention back to him. He raises his hands, I notice the blood on them. My anger spikes and my stomach churns. I point my gun at his leg and shoot. Fuck it, one hole won't hurt. The piece of fucking shit screams his head off, and falls to the filthy ground clutching his leg. I'm lucky to hear Sergio yell my name over this piss ant's cries. Standing over him, I jam my foot on his leg and apply pressure as he screams out in pain.

"Shut the fuck up. This is nothing compared to what's going to happen to you."

"Capo Bastone, it's not Miss Katherine."

What the fuck? That gets my attention. I look over and see a half-naked girl in Sergio's arms. She's beaten, dirty, and covered in blood. I slowly approach the petite brown haired girl in Sergio's arms, and watch as her eyes shift from me to Joey. There is so much fear in her deep brown eyes, I can only imagine what this piece of shit has done to her. I step in her line of sight, so she doesn't have to look at Joey again. I place my hand on her.

"Shhh, it's ok he can't hurt you anymore. He'll never touch you again." She gazes at me while weighing my words. Then, she nods, grips Sergio tighter, and I notice her knuckles turn white. I need to know if Kat was here with her.

"Can you tell me if a redheaded woman was here"

She shakes her head, and I notice her trembling. I'm concerned she is in shock. Sergio must be too because he slips his coat off and wraps it around her. He pulls her a bit closer into his chest, and when we look at each other, I see the possessive glare in his eyes. Our attention is drawn back to the girl when she speaks. I have to lean in because her voice is soft, and raspy.

"No one e-e-else w-was here," She sobs out.

"Fuck," I growl. *Fuck, where is she?*

At the sound of my angry voice, the girl flinches in Sergio's arms and huddles closer into his chest. I feel bad, but fuck it, I need to find my woman.

"I promise we won't hurt you, what's your name?"

"K-kirsty."

"How old are you Kirsty?"

"Twenty-five." Her voice is a little stronger now, and she looks between me and Sergio.

Maybe she can give me some answers now she knows we won't hurt her. I look toward Sergio and he nods in understanding.

"Tesoro mio, I need you to tell me what happened. How did you get here?" Sergio speaks softly and I raise an eyebrow at the endearment he used.

She opens her mouth to answer, when Joey screams out. Kirsty cowers in Sergio's arms.

My attention is drawn back to the asshole.

"She won't tell you shit if she knows what's good for her."

"Sergio, we need to get home. Take her in the car with you and get Doc to meet you at the house. I'm going to tie this piece of shit up and throw him in the van. I'll take him to the docks, get Dom to meet me there."

Sergio nods, tightens his arms around the sobbing girl and whispers in her ear as he heads from the warehouse.

Once they have left, I turn and look at the piece of shit crying on the floor like a bitch. Fuck, I need answers, and I need to know where the fuck my girl is. NOW! Striding over to the fireplace, I grab an old rusted fire poker. I wonder if he used this on the girl, I noticed a couple of burn marks on her arms. Hmm, I wonder if he would like the same treatment? Placing the poker into the fire, I hold it there waiting for it to turn red hot. When I look over my shoulder, his eyes are wide with fear, and he tries to scurry back on his ass while holding his leg. I look back at the poker and watch as it glows red. When I think it's hot enough to do what I want, I take it out, turn and stalk back toward him. He scampers away from me until his back hits the wall.

"Nowhere to go now, cazzo."I lower the hot poker to the gunshot wound on his leg, he screams, but no-one can hear him. I raise the poker and wait for him to stop screaming. "I can't have you bleeding out before the boss has a chance to *speak* with you."

"You may as well kill me now, I ain't telling you shit," he spits out while gritting his teeth against the pain.

"Oh, trust me, you will die. But, like I said, the boss wants to speak to you first. You *really* fucked up when you went after his fiancé, and tried to kill his kids. There is no coming back from that, and then you fucked up again by coming after my girl."

"I didn't touch your girl. I wanted to, but Billy wanted her for himself and you don't argue with him."

"Who the fuck is, Billy? And, where the fuck are they?"

His eyes widen when he realizes what he's let slip, but he doesn't say another word.

"Fuck, time to go, you piece of shit. The Boss will be waiting for you." I see the fear in his eyes, when I mention the boss. Dragging him to his feet, I pull him out of the warehouse to the van and throw him into the back. One way or another, I *will* get the answers I want. I *will* find my woman.

Chapter Sixteen

Katherine

I splutter, and gasp for breath, when cold water hits my face. The previous images of shadowed, dark brown eyes and an easy smile vanish as I'm brought back to the present. My head is spinning with pain, and confusion, wondering how the hell I ended up like this - again! I lift my head to see Ashley, standing in front of me with a water bottle in her hand.

"What time is it?" I swallow the tiny bit of saliva in my mouth, and lick my lips, trying to capture some of the water droplets still there.

Glancing around, I see we are in a dimly lit, barely furnished living room. The wallpaper is old, yellowed, and torn in places. Looking down, I see the dirty green, worn carpet, and note the filthy mattress in the corner. *Where the fuck am I?*

"Time to wake up," Ashley says, snapping my attention back to her. She sits in a chair opposite me. I wriggle my hands, and feel the rope cutting into my wrists. I have no idea how long I have been here.

I remember leaving Gwen and Harry's place, and heading toward Newcastle Mall. Someone grabbed me from behind, shoved a bag over my head, and I felt the burning prick of a needle in my neck. Then nothing. Darkness.

I have come to a couple of times when Ashley splashed water on my face, and opened my eyes to find her sitting in front of me. She glares at me with the same disgust she always has when she looks at me, but it's not long before darkness overtakes me again.

"How long have I been here?" I feel sluggish, my tongue feels too big for my mouth, and I speak really slowly. I look at Ashley again, and try to focus my eyes. *Fuck, what is wrong with me?* Ashley laughs and it echoes in my already pounding head, then I notice, her face is all bruised up. *What the hell happened to her?*

"Don't worry your head will be clear soon."

"What the fuck did you do to me?"

"Oh, nothing compared to what you deserve."

"What do you mean? What the hell have I ever done to you to deserve this? I've tried to be a good sister, I've tried for so many years."

She shrugs. "Does there have to be a reason?"

"Yes, I need to know. I don't understand why you hate me so much."

She ponders my words for a moment, I watch as she gets to her feet and turns away from me. Her shoulders rise and fall on a breath before she spins back around and takes her seat.

"When we were growing up, you seemed to have mummy wrapped around your little finger. I knew you were her favorite, no matter what I did. You were her good girl, racing to tell mum every time I did something wrong. It was like you constantly had to be the centre of attention, even if it meant I suffered. But, I dealt with it, because I had daddy. He always had time for me." She smiles as if remembering, but it quickly passes and her scowl returns. "Then, one day something changed, and daddy stopped doing things with me." She pauses, and sneers at me, like I'm shit on her shoes before going on. "You took my daddy away from me, he was mine and because of you, mum made him leave. I was his princess, but as we got older, he paid less attention to me, and more to you. He used to tell me, because I was getting older, you needed him more. We used to do everything together. He would read me stories, play games with me, come into my room late at night and lay with me. I felt safe, loved, I was his princess. So, because of you, I had to do what I did."

She stares off into the distance, tears flow down her face, and for the first time since we were little, I see something in her eyes besides hatred. I see sadness there. Oh, God is she saying dad touched her? My stomach churns at the thought, and I hold back what I want to say, because I don't want to think about it.

"What do you mean when you say you had to do what you did?"

She wipes the tears streaming from her eyes and attempts to compose herself.

"The last night daddy came to my room, he told me we couldn't do this anymore, and you needed him now. I cried and begged him not to stop loving me, but he wouldn't listen." The expression on her face now is one of pure evil, and hatred so strong, I never thought it was possible. "That's when I knew you had gotten your claws into him, so I had to make him see leaving me was a mistake. I printed off some photos he took of us together, and I showed mum. She got angry, and I knew she was jealous of the love we shared. Later that night, her and dad fought, and the next morning he was gone. Don't you see I wouldn't have had to do it if you had left him alone. He was mine, and I knew you were jealous of our love, just like mum."

Holy fucken shit, this bitch has lost her fucking mind. She is sick, and twisted, and needs fucking help.

"And, then when we got older and mum made us move, you tried to take another man away from me. Because you couldn't stop trying to ruin my life, I vowed to make you pay, and take everything you ever cared about away. I wanted to make you want to end it all, but you wouldn't take the hint, and I'm sick of waiting. So, this time I'll do it my fucking self. I wouldn't have had to do it this way, if you'd done it yourself, but you couldn't make shit

155

easy, could you? You have to always think you're something, when I know you are nothing. I planned for you to suffer long and slow, like I have been all these years. So, I started with the one person who was close to your heart."

God no, this can't be happening, is she telling me she had Brooklyn hurt?

"By the look in your eyes, I'm guessing you know who I'm talking about." She laughs and clucks her tongue before going on. "Poor little Brooklyn, so trusting and naïve, actually believed Darren could like her."

"What did you do?"

She checks her watch before going on. "I guess we have time for this little story too. When mom forced us to move, I was upset because I knew I had to leave Mathew behind. I wouldn't be able to see him every day. When I told him it was your fault, and I wanted to teach you a lesson, he suggested we should teach you a lesson by taking Brooklyn away. So, he spoke to his brother, Darren, and explained what was happening. So, you see, I knew what they were doing."

"You knew, and you still stayed with that piece of shit?"

She stands, and with one quick motion, slaps me so hard across the face, I taste blood in my mouth. *Fuck.*

"You, stupid bitch, his brother was the one who raped and killed those other women. Matt loved me, and only me," she screams at me and paces in front of me.

"Everything was going to plan, I got you away from her the night Darren raped her, and we thought we had succeed in removing her from your life. Darren had moved

156

her into his house and made sure she didn't have contact with you. But, then you came and took her, and that little bitch, away. Somehow you managed to screw things up again, so we planned to end this once and for all. But, then you had Matt killed."

She stops pacing and stares at me with tears in her eyes. "You couldn't stop yourself from taking my man away from me, you ruined my life. You just don't know when to stop, do you? I'm not allowed to be happy, am I? You just keep taking everything from me. So, when your Italian mob friends found you, and got you away from Darren, it was the last straw. I knew I had to do something myself before you took anything else away from me. So, when Antonio wouldn't leave you alone, fuck that man was obsessed with you, it didn't matter where you were, he was always there watching over you. So, I had no choice, I had to take matters into my own hands. I had him arrested." She points to the bruises on her face. "You still don't get it, do you? Why should I let you be happy, when you ruin everything for me?"

"How did you do this?" Tears run over my cheeks and drip from my chin. She's done all this, every single thing. She got Antonio arrested by accusing him of hitting her.

"It was easy. I contacted my mate, Billy, and he was more than willing to help me as long as I allowed him to play with you first."

"What does that mean?" Fuck, why is this happening to me? Everything she's saying is making my head spin. Darren, the rape, the kidnapping, everything she is saying brings it all back. God, this is all my fault, maybe I should just let her end it. I close my eyes, and try to fight the darkness pulling me under. That's when I hear Antonio's deep voice pushing through the dark thoughts. *You're a survivor, Kitten. Fight baby, push through. You were made for me, don't leave me. I need you like the air that I breathe.*

Fighting the darkness, I repeat his words in my head. "You did this, not me, Ashley. You need fucking help. We are blood, why would you do this? We're family, where is your loyalty? You were supposed to love me."

Ashley laughs like a lunatic before squatting in front of me. "Tell me something, little *sister*," she says sickly sweet. I flinch away from her touch as she pushes my hair from my face. "You write in that diary nearly every damn day, does it make you feel better to pour your heart out? Or does it just make you that bit more pathetic?" She laughs before going on. "You could have made this so much easier on yourself. You had a choice, the opportunity so many times, and nobody would have gotten hurt, but you keep trying to fight the inevitable. It doesn't matter how much you fight, Katherine, it doesn't change who you are. You're pathetic and weak, I'm amazed someone like Antonio was ever interested in you."

"He loves me." My voice is soft, unsure. I feel like a little girl again, cowering in a corner, wondering why she is doing this to me. But, finally, I know the reasons. Getting to her feet she bends over and laughs at me.

"You think I should feel sad for you? I don't. You deserve everything that has happened, and everything that is going to happen."

"Have you finished your story time now Ash, is she ready for me?" A deep voice echoes, and a man steps from the shadows of the hallway.

I suck in a deep breath, something about that voice is familiar. I know that voice, but from where, I don't know. My head is fuzzy, I can't think clearly. I just cannot remember.

"Yeah, she's ready, but remember to call out once you've had your fun. I want to be here when she finally takes her last breath. Oh, and Katherine, you want loyalty, you should have got a fucken puppy." Ashley laughs like she's just made the best joke ever, and leaves the room.

I close my eyes, as more tears fall. I jiggle my hands, trying to free them from the rope. I have managed to loosen it a bit, while she was talking, and I can still feel the gun hidden in the waistband of my pants. If I can loosen the rope a little more, I can reach it.

"Oh, and Katherine, don't fight him. Take your punishment like a good girl," she calls out before I hear a door close.

I see the man looking at me from across the room, he licks his lips and rubs his hands over his crotch. My stomach churns at the look of lust in his eyes.

"We're going to have some fun, I have been waiting for this for a while now. Oh, and I like them feisty so feel free to fight me."

"Don't fucking touch me, you piece of shit," I spit out.

He laughs as he stalks toward me.

Chapter Seventeen

Antonio

"Aaaarrrrgggghhhhhh." Joey's muffled screams filter through the thick cloth jammed in his mouth.

"Let me know if I'm doing this wrong, will you?" Dom chuckles as he cuts yet another finger from his hand with a pair of shears. "Joey, you're running out of fingers here, are you sure you don't want to spill your guts?" Dom taunts as he walks around the table Joey is strapped down to in his underwear. "You tried to take my Angel, and my children, away from me. Then, you let that psycho bitch, Janet take your keys to break into my house. You tried to have me whacked." Dom shears off another finger. "Demetri, take the gag out of his mouth. Let's see if he's got anything to say."

I lean against a wooden bench holding an assortment of knives, all of them razor sharp, and other pain causing implements. Joey struggles against the ropes holding him in place, it's futile. Even if he did manage to escape the ropes like a *Houdini*, he isn't going anywhere. Blood drips to the floor, and my mind pictures the blood coating Kristy's body in the warehouse.

I shiver when I think about the possibility of Kat suffering somewhere right now. Anger courses through me, I can't stand back and watch anymore. We have been here for over an hour, and every minute wasted, is more time away from my girl. Sergio has already managed to get answers concerning the girl from the warehouse, turns out a guy named, Billy gave her to him as payment for drugs. What asshole piece of shit would trade a woman to pay off a debt?

Sergio was pissed and sliced Joey's chest to pieces, not enough to kill him, but enough to cause him pain. I have never seen him behave that way before, usually it's my job to torture and get answers. It seems something has sparked between him, and the girl so, I was happy to give him the pleasure of cutting this piece of shit.

I look around the warehouse we are in at the docks, and see the disgust in Demetri, Nico, and Johnny's eyes as they glare at Joey. They're almost as pissed as me, the difference is, their girl isn't still missing.

Turning my attention back to Dom, I see the smirk on his lips as he positions the shears on another finger. "Traditore della famiglia"(Betrayer of the family) He closes the blades, detaching the digit, before turning to pick up a knife. He studies it closely, and weighs it in his hand, while Joey's screams echo of the walls.

Dom nods at me and I step toward Joey, his eyes widen with fear. I take the offered knife from my boss, and run the tip from the base of Joey's throat, down the centre of his body to hover just above his groin. The asshole's whimpers are doing nothing to gain my sympathy, they only fuel my need to get answers.

"How did you get Kat's backpack?" The backpack on the front seat of the van was found to have Kat's belongings in it.

"She gave it to me," he wheezes.

"Who, Ashley?"

"Yessss," he hisses when the blade glides over one of the many fresh cuts on his chest. For now, I will torment him, make him wonder when it will be his dick the knife slices off.

"How the fuck do you know Ashley?" I trail the knife back up his chest.

"She use to get her drugs off me."

"Where are they now?"

"I don't know." I drag the knife back down his body, and his eyes widen with my next words.

"Wrong answer, asshole." With a quick flick of the wrist, I slice the knife over both ankles. Demetri jams the cloth back into his mouth, and holds it in place until he stops screaming.

"One more time, you know how this works, where the fuck did Ashley take her?"

"To an old apartment building in the Junction where we use to go to get high."

"Where? ADDRESS!" I'm over the fucking games, I bring the knife up, and slice across his wrist. He screams out the address and I look toward Dominic.

"Joey, you been very helpful. So helpful in fact, I'm going to put you out of your misery without cutting off your dick. Antonio." Dominic holds out his hand, and I pass him the knife. I'm ready to finish this, and go get my girl.

"Boss, I was high. I didn't know what Janet had planned, I didn't mean for your family to get hurt. Please, Boss, don't kill me. I swear I'll do whatever you want from now on."

Pure disgust, mixed with anger, a look I have only seen a handful of times before, settles over Dominic's face before he raises the knife and studies the blade. Light glints off the blade as blood drips from it to the floor. Then, in a flash, he brings his arm down, slices the fucking assholes throat and shuts him up. The piece of shit's life is finally ended.

Dom drops the knife to the floor, and Nico hands us both a cloth to clean the blood from our hands. "Antonio, let's go get your girl. Demetri you're with us. Nico and Johnny clean this mess up," Dominic orders before we rush toward the car. I need to find my girl.

Staring through the tinted windows of the car, I watch as the sun slowly slips behind the clouds. It represents my mood, the way I'm feeling right now. Without Kat, there would be no hope of any more light in my life.

I turn toward Dom who is sitting beside me. "Boss, she's mio luce del sole (my sunshine). I can't lose her."

"Fanculo. Si." He nods.

I know I don't have to say anything else, because he understands exactly how I feel. It's only been a couple of weeks since we were racing to find his girls and he felt the same way as I do right now. Fuck, why does this shit keep happening? My girl has been through enough in her life, how much more can she take before she gives into the darkness? *No, I won't allow that to happen! I won't fucking allow my Kitten to give up, and leave me.*

I allowed the darkness to consume me for so long, and I had learnt to live with it. But, then, Kat came along, my Kitten, and everything changed. She loved me, and showed me, there was a light at the end of the tunnel. That same light awaits her, at the end of her tunnel, and I will not let her turn away from it. Kitten is mine, and I *will* get her back!

"Antonio, we will find her." Dominic interrupts my thoughts and some of my resolve slips away. They are the same words I said to him a few weeks ago. We got lucky last time, but what if this time, we're not?

Demetri pulls the car to a stop at the address we were given by Joey. It's an old apartment building; run down, windows smashed, litter everywhere, and neglected lawns. I leap from the car and sprint up the cracked footpath which leads to a glass door. The place is typical of a hangout for the local drug users.

I burst through the door with Dominic and Demetri, hot on my heels. We take the filthy stairs two at a time, hurrying to the fifth floor, where Joey said he and Ashley hang out. As we get closer, I hearing screaming followed by a loud bang. *Fuck, I know that sound. It's a gunshot.*

I'm frantic by the time I set foot onto the fifth floor and look around for Apartment 5E. As soon as I find it, I sprint down the hall, pull the gun from my waistband and kick in the door. I stop in my tracks when the barrel of a gun is pushed into my chest.

"Fuck, Kitten, it's me."

She realizes immediately who she has the gun pointed at, and drops it to the floor. A smile plays over her lips, but tears flow from her eyes.

"Antonio," she sobs as she throws herself into my chest. I hold her close, and thank Christ she is in one piece. I look over her head to see who she has shot.

"Figlia di madre," I growl.

"What is it, Antonio?" Dominic asks as he steps up beside me.

"Pezza di merda polizia," Dom spits out when he sees what I do.

Another loud bang sounds and Kat screams. I dive to the floor with her held tight in my arms. Gunshots ricochet around the room and ring in my ears. When the shooting finally stops, I move back to check Kat is not hurt. My heart thumps in my chest when I see the blood covering her shirt.

"Where are you hurt, Kitten," I yell while running my hands over her. *Where is the blood coming from? Fuck. Where is she hurt?*

"FUCK! Antonio, it's not me. I'm not bleeding."

Her hand raises to my shoulder, I feel light headed as she pushes me to the ground, and applies pressure. I look up to see tears streaming over her cheeks.

"Antonio, you need to hold on. Y-you can't leave me, not now. Please, Antonio. Please baby, stay with me."

I hear the panic in her voice and try to reassure her. "I'm not going anywhere, Kitten." I reach up and stroke the tears away. Fuck my shoulder is burning.

"Dominic, please help him." Kitten is screaming.

All I want to do is sleep. Why won't they let me sleep?

Demetri grabs hold of Kat and tries to drag her away from me. I growl at him for touching my girl and try to get up. Dom puts his hand on my chest and pushes me back down to the floor. I'm not having any of it, I want my girl by my side. "Stop fucking struggling with me, brother, let me fucking help you. Demetri has her."

I quit fighting, I'm too weak. Dom puts pressure on my shoulder, but I don't look at him. My eyes are firmly on my girl. Even crying, bleeding, and bruised, she is fucking gorgeous.

"Who the fuck shot me?" I ask weakly.

"Her sister, Ashley."

Fanculo figlio di puttana (fuck, son of a bitch). "Did you get her?"

"No Lei scappo"(she escaped). Dom is pissed, I can feel the anger coming off him in waves.

"The Ventosa di gola polizia (cock sucker police) who took my girl, is he dead?"

"Si," Dominic nods and looks away. I assume he is checking out the piece of shit, more than likely, lying dead on the floor.

It's the same figlio di puttana who touched my girl, when the cops arrested me. A fucken police officer.

"Miss Katherine, do you know his name?" Demetri asks.

"Ashley said his name was, Billy."

My eyes are getting heavy, and I can't concentrate on what's being said. I allow the darkness to draw me under, thanking fucking Christ, my girl is alive, and safe.

Chapter Eighteen

Katherine

I watch the water creep up onto the sand before it gets sucked back into the swell of the waves. I hear the water splash against the rocks nearby soothing my soul. I look up at the blue sky dotted with white fluffy clouds, and breath in the fresh ocean air. Looking back down at my diary I reread my current entry while I wiggle my toes in the sand.

Dear Diary,

It's been two weeks since I was taken, and Antonio was shot. My world tilted on its axis when I heard why Ashley hated me as much as she did. It literally blew my mind to learn our dad, the one who was supposed to protect us, started it all. It took me a while, and hours of talking with Brooklyn, to realize it wasn't my fault. It scared the shit out of me to confess to Brooklyn, to explain everything that had happened to her was because of me. A lot of tears were involved. I was so worried she would hate me, not that I would have blamed her. After all, Ashley was my sister so, I kind of feel, none of it would have happened if it wasn't for me. Brooklyn insisted, everyone makes their own choices in life, Ashley was sick, and needed help, it wasn't my fault.

Antonio and Dominic had been looking high and low for my sister until about a week ago. That was when we got the news, Ashley had been found dead of a drug overdose. I was sad, because she was my sister. I cried when I recalled the good memories we once shared. When we were little, it seemed we lived a perfect life with dreams of fairy tales, and kissing a frog, to find our Prince Charming. But, I was also relieved, because she couldn't hurt anybody anymore. It was like the shadow I felt lurking for such a long time, was finally gone. I could move forward and live again.

I close my diary, place it on the sand beside me, lean back on my elbows and take in the sight of the setting sun in the distance. I smile when I sense him sit down beside me and draw me into his side.

"Kitten, what's going on in that head of yours? " He places a soft kiss to my temple.

"How did you find me, Stud?"

"Kitten, there is no place you can be, without me finding you. Haven't I proved that enough during our time together?" He chuckles and draws me closer into his side.

"Thank you," I whisper

"For what?"

"For never giving up on me. For not trying to fix me. For letting me do it myself."

"Kitten, you don't need to be fixed. You're perfect the way you are."

"Flaws and all, you mean?"

"Katherine," he breathes out, and I look at him. He never uses my full name, unless he's serious. "Your flaws are what make you who you are, who I love. I would take you over anything else in this life. The fire living inside you is what got my attention to begin with, but it was your heart and strength, which kept me coming back for more."

I sniff back the tears and watch my toes wiggling in the sand. Antonio places his fingers under my chin, draws my face to his, and leans forward to plant a soft kiss on my lips.

"You are mio luce del sole, Kitten. After my momma died, I lived in a constant state of darkness, until you walked into my life."

I remember him mentioning a while ago that his parents had died, but he never told me what happened. All I know is, he was adopted by Dominic's uncle, Santino, when his parents passed away.

"Tell me what happened to her?"

He stares out at the water, and watches the waves as the sun finally sets. A blanket of black surrounds us.

"When I was eleven years old, my papa died of a heart attack. It devastated momma, I used to hear her crying at night, and I knew her heart shattered that day. My father was her soul mate. Momma did the best she could, got a part time job at the local deli and we were getting by. We were slowly putting our life back together." He blows out a deep breath before continuing. "I came home from school one day, and when I walked in, a man was standing over my momma. She was lying on the floor crying, naked, and bloody. He was doing up his pants. I froze, I didn't know what to do. Then, he looked over and saw me. He laughed, and said if I didn't keep my mouth shut, he would kill her next time while I watched. I ran to my momma's side, and tried to cover her body with mine. He laughed at me, and told me, eventually I would learn to be a man and he would teach me - men don't cry. I didn't know what to do. I looked into my momma's brown eyes, so much like mine, and they were pleading with me not to argue. I looked back up at the man, he wasn't a big man, but bigger than me. A menacing scar, running down the side of his face caught my eye. He was scary to a boy my age, and I nodded my agreement. I will never forget the sick, twisted smirk which pulled at his lips."

Fuck. I wrap my arms around his waist, and peer through my lashes at him. I notice how glassy his eyes are, it hurts to see him hurting this way.

"I'm so sorry. I know it's painful, you don't have to continue."

"Si, I do." He draws me into his lap.

"Your arm," I protest.

"It's fine, and I need to hold you when I tell you the rest."

I nod, he exhales and keeps going.

"For almost a year, I endured what think of as hell. I was beaten, tied to chairs, and placed in a wooden trunk for days on end with no food or water. When I argued back, or disagreed with the asshole, he'd threaten to take my momma away from me. After the first day, when I came home and found my momma laid out on the floor, nothing was ever the same. I learned to stop asking questions pretty quickly."

Antonio sighs deeply.

"After spending God only knows how long in that wooden trunk, I was hungry and light headed. I didn't want to be forced in there again. So, I decided to give in, and let him believe I had submitted to him. My momma had become a shell of the person she once was. Not once did she speak out of turn, as he would put it. She was afraid of what would happen to her, I guess. Every time I fought him, I could see the struggle she had with herself, to stop what he would do to me. Maybe I should have hated her for what happened, but I didn't. She had brought the wrong man home, become a victim like me, and I wanted to protect her.

I heard her cries and screams every night, he would tell her to shut up, and give him what he was owed. I didn't know what that meant, and I didn't care. I just knew I had to do something to stop him, but what was I supposed to do? I was twelve years old, what could I do? Then, one night, when I was hiding under my bed and hoping he wouldn't come for me, I came up with a plan. I just had to figure out how to pull it off."

Another long sigh.

"On the way home from school the next day, I walked past the old Deli where my momma used to do odd jobs.

She had mentioned, some powerful men met there to talk and drink coffee. I saw them at one of the tables and offered my services to them. At first, they laughed at me, and told me to go home and grow up. To come back when I was older. But, I was determined to free my momma so, every day for a month, I stopped by and offered myself to them. Finally, one day, they took me seriously and introduced me to a man named Santino. He took me aside, and asked why I was so determined to join them. He said this was not the path I needed to travel down, it wasn't the right life for me. I explained what had been happening for the past year, and watched a million emotions cross his face. By the time, I had finished explaining, he understood how desperate I was. It seemed my persistence paid off in my favour, he said the Big Boss would stop at the Deli the next day."

Antonio takes my face in his hand and kisses me gently.

"The next day, when the Big Boss showed up, he looked me up and down, shook his head and turned away. I had a feeling that was it, and my hopes of saving my momma, were lost. Then, Santino stepped up, and spoke in The Boss' ear as I watched. The Boss nodded, and I knew at that moment, I would do anything to save my momma, even if it meant being tied to the mob for the rest of my life."

He blows out a deep breath, and I feel it wash over me.

"The Boss ordered Santino and a few other guys to take me home, he instructed them to *fix* the situation. You need to understand, although the mob is known for their illegal dealings, they have a strict code of conduct they follow. One of those rules, is to never cause harm to women or children, so, to say they were pissed is an understatement. Apparently, the guy who had basically controlled our lives for over a year, was a man the mob had been after for a while. He was a loan shark from another family who had ripped them off. I later found out, my papa had a huge gambling debt when he died. Apparently, him being dead didn't matter, it was now our responsibility to pay it off. Once everything was sorted, and the mob took care of the piece of shit, I did small jobs for Santino. He told me there was no debt owed to them, that my momma and I had already paid enough. But, for me, he gave us back our lives that day, and I was determined to repay them. So, I would wash their cars, hang their coats, basically anything I could. As I got older, I did other jobs for them. I can't go into detail, but I'm pretty sure you get the picture. I thought my momma was getting better, she started to smile again. God she had a beautiful smile, and when she laughed, it was better than any music you could have heard. Usually when I came home from the deli, she'd be in the kitchen making dinner, but this day I couldn't find her. I went upstairs to her bedroom thinking she might be sick. Her bedroom door was closed, and when I knocked, there was no answer. I was worried about her, so I opened the door to go in. My worst nightmare was in front of me, my momma had cut her wrists and bled to death. I couldn't believe what I was seeing, I thought my momma was healing and getting better. I realized when I was older, she had built a wall around herself, and was an expert at showing the world, she was fine. Inside, she was drowning in her demons. Santino took me in and gave me the Grasso name."

I feel his tears hit my forehead, his breathing quickens and I'm lost for words. My big, strong man has deep hurt I may never be able to heal, but I can be here for him, just like he is here for me.

"Antonio, I love you."

He presses a kiss to my forehead, and we sit in silence in own little bubble while waves crash against the rocks, and the moon shines across the water.

Chapter Nineteen

The Next day

Antonio

My arm is wrapped around my woman's waist when we stride into Dominic's the next day, I feel content for the first time in a long time. I would rather have stayed in bed all morning, hmmm, the things I could have done to my lady, but I have to talk to Dom about the Chinese fucker in prison. So much has happened, it slipped my mind. Now things have settled down, and my girl is safe, we need to get this shit sorted out. Kat and I pause in the entry when we hear Dom's raised voice. He sounds pissed. Who the fuck is he yelling at?

We hurry toward where the voice is coming from in the kitchen, and stop at the doorway. Brooklyn is standing behind the kitchen bench with her arms folded over her chest, and Dom is pacing in front of her.

"Brooklyn, you will tell me what the fuck I want to know. NOW!" Dom shouts.

"Don't you fucking shout at me, Dominic Grasso." Brooklyn slams her hands on the kitchen bench and leans forward as far as her belly will allow.

"Did she just full name him?" Kat whispers in shock.

I nod, and I'm also in shock.

Dom stops pacing, slams his hands down on the bench, and leans toward his fiancé. Their noses are almost touching. "Brooklyn, I will find out. Tomorrow I'm going to pick my daughter up from school..."

Brooklyn cuts him off. "Dom, you're overreacting, it was just a little kiss."

Whoa! What the fuck? Did some figlia di madre kiss the boss's woman? No wonder he's fucking pissed.

"I don't give a fuck. No-one, and I mean, *no-one* touches what's mine!"

I hear footsteps on the stairs, and look over my shoulder to see a smiling Evie.

"Zio,"(uncle) she says as she runs to me. She started calling me uncle not long after I was shot, and I love hearing it. Picking her up, I sit her on my hip.

"Aunty Kat, Daddy is really mad."

"I can tell, Dollface."

"Princess, come give your papa a hug." Dom holds out his arms, I set her on the ground, and she runs to her papa.

Dom pushes stray curls off her face and kisses her forehead. "Princess, you tell that boy, if he kisses you or touches you again, your dad..."

That sets me back on my heels. Some little punk kissed our Evie. I clear my throat before adding, "and, uncle Antonio will come to your school with your papa."

Brooklyn shakes her head, and bites her lip. She's trying hard not to laugh. I scowl, Evie being kissed is no laughing matter. I glance down at Kat and see she is doing the same thing. I give her a squeeze and when she looks up, I frown. I don't think there is anything fucking funny about this at all.

"Dominic, seriously she's in preschool. You can't go threaten little kids."

"You think? Just watch me, Angel. Nobody, and I mean *nobody,* touches my Principessa."

Brooklyn throws her arms in the air. "There is absolutely no talking to you, I don't know why I told you in the first place. I should have known you would react this way."

Brooklyn turns away.

Dom puts Evie down, and she runs off to play. He rounds the bench and gathers his fiancé to him.

"Angel, don't be angry at me." Dom's voice is low, but not low enough that we don't hear him. Brooklyn turns in his arms and places her hands against his chest.

"Big Man, it was only a sweet little kiss between two small children. There is no need to get all caveman about it. They're just *kids.*"

"That's no fucking excuse," I growl.

Brooklyn narrows her eyes at me, and if looks could kill, I'd be six feet under by the end of the day.

"Not helping, Stud." Kat nudges me in the side with her elbow causing me to grunt. I lick my lips, and my dick twitches, when she swings those fucking hips as she walks away. She settles herself on the floor with Evie.

Dom's voice has me looking back toward him and Brooklyn. "I have to deal with some business, this conversation isn't over Angel." Dom bends forward, and takes Brooklyn in a deep kiss.

"That's what you think, Big Man. The matter is so closed, the door is nailed shut." Brooklyn laughs as she steps from Dom's arms.

He walks away, cursing in Italian.

"Babydoll, do you have a boyfriend?" Kat asks Evie, while they color in.

"Kat." Dom warns as he storms over to me.

The tone of his voice with my woman is to get my back up, but I notice the look on my Kitten's face, I realize she is trying to get a rise out of Dom.

It's Dom's turn to throw his hands in the air. "Antonio, we have shit to do. Follow me."

I nod, follow him from the room and head toward his office.

The girl's laughter floats through the air as it follows

"What the fuck is going on Boss?" I take a seat in front of his desk while he closes the door behind him.

"I can't believe some punk kid kissed my daughter. I overheard Brooklyn talking with Evie before you guys turned up. I swear to Christ, they are trying to kill me, brother. Fanculo," he growls. He pulls a folder from his desk drawer and flips it open.

"Some shit went down while you were inside."

I nod. "I remember you mentioning something was happening when we spoke on the phone while I was locked up."

"Yeah, it was no use giving you details while you were in there. The ghost shadows got the shipment, which we were already aware of, but apparently, it was short. We need to work out why. Theo and Nico looked into it, and came up with a name."

He slides the folder across the desk to me. I look down to see a photo of the piece of shit cop who Kat killed. "Okay, so he's dead. Problem solved." Dom is shaking his head, so I wait for him to continue.

"That cop was dirty as fuck, but he had connections. He was working with the Ghost Shadows, until he ripped them off."

"It's not our fucking problem, they had the piece of shit on retainer."

"Si, but it does affect us when someone takes from us. Billy Boy wasn't working alone, and we need to find whoever his partner was. I believe the girl you saved in the warehouse may be in danger."

"How is she doing?"

"Sergio, said she is getting there, but she's scared shitless and refuses to talk about anything. He has her at the safe house. We need to work out who that piece of shit's partner was, and fast."

"What about his cop buddy who put the cuffs on me?".

"No. He was the first one we thought of. Theo did a complete background check, but he comes up clean"

"Fuck, that would have been too easy."

"Si, Theo is investigating every lead he can find, and Nico is tracking down anybody who had contact with Billy. They are also trying to find out who else knew about the fucking shipment."

"One of the Ghost Shadow pricks in jail, warned you better watch your back. I'm going to get Alfio to search why he got locked up, and see when he's getting out. I'll pay him a visit, no-one threatens my brother."

"Si, how's your arm?"

"Bene, Boss"

"Anything else we need to discuss?"

"Si, Katherine's father. Everything that has happened to our women, appears to link back to him. I think we need to pay him a visit."

"Si, I believe so too. Brooklyn has mentioned he was an asshole." Dom nods and I notice him flexing his hands into fists.

Yeah, my feelings exactly. I think he's overdue for some man on man talk. Karma's a bitch, especially coming from us.

Katherine

When the guys leave the room, I stand, walk over to Brooklyn in the kitchen, and lean against the bench. "Dollface, I can't believe you full named him. A fucking mafia boss!" I laugh.

"He's overreacting. For fuck sake, it was one little kiss. The little boy chased her around the playground, and when he caught her, he kissed her cheek. I think it's cute." She rubs her baby bump, and I reach over and give it a little rub too.

"So how are you holding up?" Brooklyn asks as she heads to the fridge.

"I'm doing a lot better. Antonio and I have talked for hours about everything that's happened. I still feel guilty, but I know she was sick, and instead of getting help, she decided to do what she did." I glance over my shoulder, and make sure Evie is still playing before turning back to my best friend and continuing. "I can't believe what my father did, and I don't understand why mom didn't call the police."

"Did he touch you?" Her voice is barely a whisper, I know it's a question she didn't want to ask.

"No, he didn't. I think when Ashley showed mom the pictures, he was forced to leave before it could happen. In her own sick, and twisted way, she saved me from him. Not that saving me would have crossed her mind considering everything she did afterward."

"Honey, none of it was your fault."

"I know." I sniff back the tears as she wraps her arms around me.

"You can't blame yourself, it will push you back into the darkness. I couldn't bear to lose you, I love you."

I nod into her shoulder and step away, brushing the tears from my face. Brooklyn pours orange juice into three glasses and passes me one.

"Enough about me, how's the girl they found in the warehouse?"

"Sergio borrowed some clothes from me, but he didn't say much. Dom said Sergio is taking care of her and Doc has been to check on her."

"Wasn't she staying here?"

"Yeah, at first. I'm not sure what happened, but Dom had her moved to a safe house. I don't know why, Dom's being pretty tight lipped about it. I feel bad, she looked as if she had been through so much, and needed a friend. I hope they figure out what happened to her and keep her safe."

"Yeah, me too. God only knows what happened to her if that piece of shit cop had anything to do with it." I blow out a breath before going on. "I know I have asked you before but how did you feel when you shot Janet?"

Brooklyn checks on Evie before she speaks. "I thought I should feel sad, but I didn't. I finally felt like I was taking control of my life again, does that make sense? For such a long time, I have blamed myself for what happened with Darren. I should have taken control, and left him sooner. When Janet threatened Dom, I knew I would never allow anyone to ruin my life again. It was her, or the man I love. I didn't hesitate and I have no regrets. I need to look to the future now, and leave the past behind. I have a great man who loves me unconditionally, a beautiful daughter, who is the happiest I have ever seen her, and possibly two precious babies on the way. I had two choices, I could either keep rerunning the past, and let it tear me down, or I could open my eyes and live in the now. I chose to let the past go and I couldn't be happier."

I think about what she's said, and I know she's right. There is no point in delving into the past, wondering 'what if', when I have everything I have ever dreamed of in front of me.

"Good point, Dollface."

"Kitten, we need to go home."

Antonio's voice interrupts us and I turn to watch him and Dominic enter the room. *Fuck my man is sexy.* Ever since he opened up to me about his mom last night, the shadows living behind his eyes have vanished. It feels good to have been able to help him.

"Why, Stud?" I'm confused, I thought we were staying for lunch

"We have plans." He looks me up and down, and I feel the lust deep into my bones.

Again, I shoot him a confused look. He winks at me with a sexy as sin smirk on his lips. My toes curl, and I know exactly what plans he has in mind.

Chapter Twenty

Katherine

I barely get a chance to open the front door before I'm pushed inside, and up against the entry wall. Antonio's lips are on mine, devouring me like I'm his next meal. I moan into his mouth when he draws my leg up to wrap around his waist. He groans when the full length of him pushes against my heated core.

The ringing of a phone pierces my lust filled head. Antonio groans and pulls away. I try to catch my breath as he pulls his phone from his pocket, and holds it to his ear.

"Che cosa,"(what) he growls into the phone.

Sliding my leg down to the ground, I stand on shaking legs. When I see Antonio's look of annoyance at being interrupted, I bite my lip to stop the giggle that wants to escape.

"Si Brother," he says gruffly. He slaps my ass when I slide past him, and head toward the stairs. *Fuck it I may as well tease him as I go.* Pulling my shirt over my head, I drop it to the floor and swing my hips as I walk.

I hear his deep growl from behind me.

"I'll meet you upstairs, stud," I toss over my shoulder. I don't miss the possessive look in his eyes, causing goosebumps to spread over my body.

I head to the closet in my bedroom, and grab the outfit I had picked out to wear for him when he was released. Hurrying to the bathroom, I strip the rest of my clothes off, and quickly pull on my outfit.

Standing in front of the mirror, I run my fingers through my hair to give it a mussed look. My red lipstick is on the sink where I left it, begging to be used. I swipe it over my swollen, pouty lips. "Kitten, is everything okay?" Antonio's deep husky voice calls out from the other side of the bathroom door.

"Everything is good, Stud. Give me a moment." I kick my discarded clothes to the side and notice my red heels sitting behind the door. *Perfect just what I need to finish the look.* Slipping them onto my feet, I blow out a deep breath and open the door.

"Holy fucken shit, luce del sole." He slams his hand over his chest.

I'll take that as a good sign.

"You like.... You look.... You are...."

I lower my eyes and play with the hem of the short skirt, I feel suddenly shy. The way he is devouring me with his eyes causes butterfly's to swarm in my belly. Placing his fingers under my chin he brings my face up to look at his.

"Fuck, Kitten. What are you trying to do to me?" He takes my hand and draws me forward. "Come out here, I want to see you better." He leads me into the bedroom, takes a couple of steps back, and sits on the edge of the bed. Then, he raises his finger in the air and twirls it around.

I turn slowly in a circle so, he can take in the sexy police outfit I picked up the last time Brooklyn and I went shopping. His eyes are smoldering, taking a few steps toward him, I stand between his spread legs, and mustering all my courage, jam one hand on my hip, pull the handcuffs from my belt and dangle them from my fingers.

"You want to play, Kitten?" His voice is deeper and huskier than normal as he runs his calloused hands up my bare legs.

"I need a new diary entry, and I thought you could help me. *Stud.*"

He gives me a puzzled look, not sure what I mean.

"I want to write about all the naughty things you are going to do to me." The words have barely left my lips when, he grips my hips, and I'm on my back on the bed. Antonio is looming above me.

"Whoa, Stud," I giggle.

"You want me to cuff you, Kitten?" His voice is thick with his Italian accent, and it sends shivers dancing down my spine. Before I can answer, he leans forward and kisses me. Then, he pulls back, and whispers against my lips "No, Kitten, I have a much better idea."

"Yeah, perno, and what's that?"

He raises a dark eyebrow at my use of the Italian name for Stud.

"Ah, my Kitten, has been learning." He taps my nose causing me to scrunch it.

Leaning back, he stares at me, runs his hands down, then back up my body until he reaches the buttons running down the middle of my outfit. He slowly unfastens them, one by one. My breathing hitches when he pushes both sides of the bodice away from my body, lowers his head and kisses my breasts through my red lacy bra. *I forgot I had that bra on. Fuck, I hope I have the matching panties on too. Snatching a quick look down, I thank the pantie gods they are matching.*

"Fanculo, Kitten you're sexy as fuck. And it's all *mine*."

He takes my mouth in a deep kiss. When we part, we're both breathing heavy. He slides from the bed, stands and gazes at me through hooded eyes. Taking his shirt off, the glint of his piercing catches my eye. I lick my lips, wanting to play with it. My eyes savor the sight of him, when he unzips his pants, and reveals his black boxer briefs. *Fuck, my man is sexy.* He bends over, and picks something up off the dressing table before slowly making his way to me.

"What's that?" I nod toward his hand as I sit up.

"I thought we could have some fun." He shows me what he has in his hand.

"With Nutella, Stud?"

"Fuck yeah, Kitten." He licks his lips.

Wow, just the thought of him smoothing chocolate spread over my body, and licking it off, has me wanting to beg him to shut up, and get on with it.

"Lay back, Kitten." Antonio chuckles when I throw myself eagerly back onto the pillows.

"As much I love this little get up, I want you naked." Before I have a chance to take my underwear off, he grips the side of my lace panties, and rips them from my body.

"Fuck, it's hot when you do that, Stud," I giggle, and sit up to take my heels off.

"Leave them on," Antonio asks.

I nod and lay back as he crawls onto the bed between my spread legs. I hear the lid on the jar click as he opens it before placing it on the nightstand. He flicks the front clasp of my bra open, and I sigh when Antonio's mouth latches onto my nipple. I shiver when he runs his finger, coated with Nutella, over the other nipple. Switching breasts, he licks, sucks and nips off the chocolate, while he coats the other nipple with Nutella.

Moaning at the sensation being created, I wriggle with delight. Every pull, lick and bite from his mouth shoots straight to my core. Releasing my breast with a soft pop, he sits back on his ankles, and runs two fingers covered in chocolate, down my chest. He reaches my clit, and rubs his fingers in circles, pulling a moan from me.

Leaning over, he laps at my body like a starved man, until he reaches my clit. He sucks forcibly, inserts one, then another finger, stretching me until he finds my g-spot. The insistent rubbing causes my body to tense up as bolts of electricity shoot through me. I fall into an orgasm so fierce, I swear it feels like I'm flying. He slides up my body, and I hum at the feel of his weight on top of me.

"Kitten, open your eyes."

I didn't even realize they were closed, opening them, I see his handsome face smiling at me. "We should do that more often, Stud," I murmur, bringing a deep laugh from him. He bends over and kisses me, I moan at my taste on his tongue.

"We haven't finished yet, Kitten."

"Oh really, what do you have in mind now?"

"I want to do it kitty style."

"Don't you mean doggy style, Stud?"

"No, I mean kitty style. Me on top, pounding into your tight heat, as you drag your nails down my back."

"Oooh, I like the sound of that." I lift up, and wrap my mouth around his piecing making him moan, his hand holds the back of my head in place. I run my nails down his back, causing him to hiss and arch into my hands.

"Fuck me, Antonio."

Leaning down, he kisses me hard. I bring my legs up, catch his boxer briefs with my heel, and drag them down until I feel his hard cock bounce free. The tip hits my clit, and I moan. Antonio also groans at the contact.

"Fuck, Kitten, I can't wait," Antonio growls, breaking the kiss

"Now, Antonio, please. Fuck me, now."

With one hard thrust, he's inside me. I groan, and my nails dig into his back just as he asked. Thrust after thrust, he pounds into me until we are both lost in the sensation between us. I'm not sure who's making more noise, but I'm soaking in every feeling he is causing to race through my body. One last thrust and he takes me over the edge with him. I feel him explode inside me, triggering more spasms to run through my body.

Chapter Twenty-One

Antonio

I stride into the living room, pick up the remote, and turn the television onto the music channel. *Cherry Pie* by *Warrant* is playing. I head to the kitchen to start on dinner.

Fuck, I still have the image of Kat standing in front of me in that sexy as fuck, police stripper outfit and those red, fuck me heels. I felt like I was going to explode in my pants before I even had a chance to touch her. Just thinking about is getting me hard all over again. I rummage through the fridge, pull out some steaks Kat had defrosting, and place them on the counter.

After taking my girl three times, she fell asleep in my arms where she belongs. Laying with her, I knew everything was finally starting to click into place, it feels fucking fantastic. I hear her come down the stairs as I grab the marinade from the cupboard.

"What are you doing, Stud?" Her sleepy voice comes from behind as she wraps her arms around me, and I feel her lips kiss the centre of my back.

Turning in her arms, I place a kiss to her forehead. She raises her head, and I kiss her soft lips.

"I'm cooking dinner tonight"

"What did I do to deserve you?"

"Kitten, take a seat, and watch me work my magic."

She smiles and drops her arms, releasing me. She takes a seat at the bench, I pull down a glass, fill it with wine, slide it toward her.

After turning back to the steaks, and unscrewing the lid of the marinade, I look back over my shoulder. I watch as she takes a mouthful of wine, closes her eyes and sighs. I chuckle, she moans and blushes when she realizes I was watching her.

"Kitten, I'm moving in." I turn back to the steaks, and hear the glass placed on the bench a little too hard.

"You're what?"

I don't give her a chance to protest. "I'm here all the time anyway. I love going to sleep with you in my arms, and waking up with you."

"I love that too." Her voice is wistful.

I turn around and lean against the bench. I look into the eyes that have held me captive since the first day I met her.

"What?"

"Nothing. I need you to sign that paper on the counter." I nod toward the paper sitting near the phone.

"What is it?" she asks as she gets to her feet and moves to the counter.

I walk up behind her and wrap my arm around her waist as she reads what's written. I hear her small gasp, dig in my pocket and pull out the diamond ring I have bought for her. I lift her hand from the counter, slip the ring onto her finger, lift it to my lips and put a forever binding kiss there. Then, I plant a small kiss to her temple and whisper in her ear, "I love you."

Placing my fingers under her chin, I turn her face toward me, bend down and kiss her on the lips.

"Antonio?"

"Si, Kitten?"

"Aren't you even going to ask me to marry you?"

I shake my head, because I am not asking anything. "Are you mine, Kitten?" I lean against the stove and fold my arms over my chest. I smirk at the way she is checking me out until her eyes finally meet mine. Her tongue darts out to lick her lips, and I feel my cock harden from the lustful look in her eyes.

"Yes?"

"Am I yours?"

"Yes," she answers and I chuckle because I swear I heard a growl in her voice.

"Then it's settled, you're mine, and I'm yours. Seems like a done deal to me."

We stare at each other for a few moments. I'm expecting her to demand I ask her properly, but instead, she moves slowly, seductively toward me. She closes the distance between us, swinging those fucking hips and I feel my inner caveman come to the surface at how sexy she looks in my shirt.

"So, you're my fiancé?" She whispers from barely a breath away, and I feel the air hit my chest.

"Si." I nod, not trusting my voice to speak

"So, shouldn't we celebrate?" She trails her nail down my chest causing goosebumps to breakout across my skin.

It's taking every bit of control I have to stand here, and not rip my shirt from her body to take what is mine. Leaning forward, she sucks my nipple bar into her mouth, and swirls her tongue around making me groan.

"Fuck, Kitten."

"That's exactly what I was thinking, Stud," she fucking purrs, as she kisses down my chest, and drops to her knees in front of me. My boxer briefs hit the floor, she runs her hand up and down my cock before slipping it into her warm wet mouth. Her tongue swirls around the tip, driving me crazy. I tangle my fingers into her hair, pull her head back, and two blue eyes stare up at me. Her mouth now full of my cock. *Fuck. She is a fucking sex Kitten.* Closing my eyes, I concentrate on the feel of her tongue, her warm mouth, she has me floating on air. I glance down and see the light, and love in her eyes. My body becomes tense, and I fall over the edge roaring her name.

Katherine

I'm engaged, holy fucking shit! I'm actually engaged, I can't believe it. Me, the girl who has wanted to do away with herself for years. I have someone who loves me deeply, who wants me to spend the rest of my life with him.

After Antonio had a mind-blowing orgasm, pun intended, he showed his appreciation by taking me to the floor and sending me over the edge three times. By the time, we were done, I was jelly legged, and gasping for air. When I was able to feel my legs again, and my head came back to earth, I left him in the kitchen to finish dinner while I came upstairs to have a shower. I can't resist grabbing my diary and telling it the good news. Sitting crossed legged on my bed, I open to a blank page.

Dear Diary,

Something happened to me today, something I could have only ever dreamed about in my wildest fantasies. Antonio proposed! Well, he didn't actually propose. He told me he was mine, and I was his, so we were getting married. How could I say no to that?

He honestly believes, I'm the light to his dark, but I think we both balance each other out. Whenever Antonio is around, it feels like I can control the demons, the darkness that has followed me for so long. I can slowly begin to heal, not just because I have the love of a good man by my side, but because I have someone I know will stand beside me, no matter what. I have Brooklyn and Evie too, I don't think I could have succeeded in fighting the darkness without them. I think I would have let it take me a long time ago, but they never stopped loving me, and made sure when I was ready, they were there to catch me.

Last night, I tried to talk to Antonio about me possibly not being able to give him a family. I told him about the diagnosis of Polycystic Ovarian Syndrome when I was eighteen. I explained everything I had found out about the condition and chances of me having a child were extremely slim. He insisted, it if turned out to be only us, it was more than enough.

He held me while I cried, but I didn't cry because he upset me. I cried because I was happy that all the secrets, the past is behind us, and we can move forward. If we aren't blessed with children, I'll be happy just having him by my side.

Because, he is my light as I am his. We will guide each other through the darkness. Together we will overcome.

Epilogue

Letter to Kat from Antonio, written during his time in jail.

My Kitten,

It's hell being in here, not having you wrapped in my arms.

I've had a hard life and never believed I deserved anything good. Still, to this day, I don't believe I deserve the love you have to give, but that isn't going to stop me from taking it. You, and that mouth of yours, have burrowed deep into my soul. Every day, we suffer and fight the darkness that tries to consume us. I thought I had already given in, allowed it to claim me, and the life I was living, was the way it was going to be. I never believed in love at first sight, or feeling a connection so deep, it takes you to the ground, but you changed all that for me.

You have survived so much already, and I hope you still have a bit more fight in you to get you through the days until I can be with you again. Because, when I get out, I will never let you go.

One lifetime with you will never be enough, but we are going to make it one hell of a lifetime. I can't promise you the dark days are over, but I sure as fuck can give you my word - you will never be alone again.

Your Stud.

Three months later

Katherine

Dear Diary,

It feels like a lifetime since I have written to you. In the past, you seemed like my only out. My only way of feeling anything. I needed you to stop the darkness from overtaking me because there was no-one I else I could turn to. But, I was wrong.

I found Antonio and he helped me believe in myself. He gave me strength. I still can't control my tongue and my sassy attitude, but Antonio says it's one of the things he loves the most about me. Months ago, he urged me to write all my wants down. He's convinced me, I deserve each and every one of them.

When you find a love that pierces your soul, you hold on with both hands, because a love like that, so strong and powerful, doesn't come around twice. Our love is like the words from the most passionate love stories ever written, and the most romantic love songs ever sung. It drips from the sky on a rainy day, and shines like the stars on the clearest nights. I'm guessing you get my drift. I like to romanticize it, because for most of my life, I believed I could kiss a thousand frogs, and never find that one person who could handle all my downfalls. Someone who would be willing to lend me their strength to help me build myself back up.

I still have dark days, but with Antonio by my side, I know when I have my broken moments he will be there for me. There will always be demons I have to fight in life, thinking I'm not good enough, pretty enough, strong enough, but every time I put that blade down, I know how much of a survivor I really am.

I didn't realize how broken I really was until I broke down in my kitchen that day with Brooklyn. My best friend, and the love of my life, knew how badly I was hurting, but they needed me to break down the walls and let them in. When I did, they were there to help me piece myself back together. I don't think I needed anyone to fix me, I needed to know I wasn't alone anymore.

I have learned, you have to fight through the tough days to get to the best days of your life. Every thought used to be a battle, every breath was a war, and until my walls tumbled, I was not going to win. So, all the fighting and pushing to be free, makes every day brighter. The smile I wear now is real. I can't hide anything behind it anymore, not that Antonio would allow me to anyway.

"Kitten, what are you doing?" I turn toward Antonio, and take him in from head to toe. When our eyes meet, I see the gleam there, and know exactly what's on his mind. After placing my diary on the nightstand, before I get a chance to blink, he's on me and taking my mouth in a deep kiss. His hand travels down my body until he's cupping my already wet core.

"Mine, Kitten," he growls into my mouth as he makes slow circles over my clit.

I pull back on a moan, and whisper against his lips. "Yours, Stud. Always yours."

Four Months Later

Dear Diary,

Today I married my best friend, my soul mate. My forever. He tells me all the time, I'm his sunshine. The light at the end of the tunnel, and no matter how dark it becomes, or how hard the fight seems, as long as we have each other, we can conquer anything thrown our way.

Today was perfect, I'm not talking about the flowers, the dress or even the cake. No, I'm talking about the man standing at the end of the aisle waiting for me. He is my light in the darkness, like the old light house helping the ships find their way home. He is the calmness that settles over the ocean after a storm.

Antonio says, I'm like that different sea shell you find washed up on the beach, and don't throw away because I'm not like anything else. Instead of throwing me back into the ocean, you take me home, and cherish me, even though I have flaws.

I sit here and watch my husband sleep. He's so handsome, and when his sleeping, the shadows don't follow him, he's peaceful.

I know I have been slack about writing in you these days but every day I'm stronger, and instead of closing myself off, and writing about the things worrying me, I open up and talk about them. It feels good to be able to do that.

Brooklyn is close to having her little boys. Yep, that's right. Dominic was right, the twins are boys and he has to be the proudest father I have ever seen. Her face lit up with love and excitement when she found out, she was over the moon with joy. Until Dominic and Antonio informed her, now they wouldn't have to step in on any other boys who tried to kiss Evie, her brothers would take care of it. Brooklyn pretended to be pissed off for like five minutes. I have to give the girl credit, she is overcoming the past, getting stronger every day, and I'm finally seeing the girl I first met. Knowing she has Dominic to help her through her dark moments is reassuring. I couldn't have wished for anyone more perfect for her, and I am so fucking proud of how far she has come. My heart is so full of love, knowing our family is growing, and getting stronger together. But, we won't rest until we all get our Happy Ever After.

So, this isn't The End.

This is only the Beginning.

Sugar Mine

Kirsty

I have lived in a constant nightmare for so long, I can't ever remember having a normal life. I was never somebody's anything besides a prisoner, a punching bag, someone's debt to pay. I was betrayed by the very people who should have loved me. I'm not sure exactly what love means anymore. Is it being asleep, and being dragged from your bed at night to be told the world I once knew was a lie? That I was only ever born to cover up someone else's mistake. A mistake that stole my life away from me.

I learnt very quickly not to trust anybody, let alone a man, but one look into a pair of midnight eyes swimming in pain, woke something inside me I thought had died a long time ago. How can one look cause so many emotions to play through my body after feeling dead inside for so long? But I don't know if I have anything else to give, I'm a shell of the girl I once was, and I don't know if I will ever be whole again.

Sugar: One touch, one look, one simple husky whispered word, and I felt the safest I had ever felt. Sergio was going to either fill the emptiness inside me or leave me gasping for air.

Sergio

Growing up surrounded by the mob, and looking like I do, means you come in handy for a lot of reasons. I learnt a long time ago, the ins and outs, and if it wasn't for Dominic Grasso, I wouldn't be breathing right now. I owe him everything, a debt I may never be able to pay. Laying my life on the line for him is the least I can do.

Looking into a pair of huge brown eyes, laced with pain, I knew I had to try and save her, even if it meant opening old wounds. You don't get too many second chances in life, so when one comes along, you don't turn a blind eye, you reach out and grab it with both hands. Kirsty is that second chance, and I will lay my life on the line to find the answers she deserves. I am big, and scary as fuck, I don't say a lot, but when she clung to me like I was her lifeline, she didn't know it at the time, but she sealed her fate and became mine to save, to protect, to love.

Sergio: I will set the world on fire to give Kirsty the peace she deserves. I will move Heaven and Earth to protect her, and I will fall to my knees to save her.

Bonus Scene which didn't make it into the book, but I thought you might enjoy it.

Katherine

"Hey, you know how when I talk to someone I like to look them in the eyes?"

"Hmmm," Antonio nods, and looks at me, like he's not quite sure where I'm going with this.

"Well, when I went to the shop this morning, I was trying to have a conversation with the assistant behind the counter, but I ended up walking away before I lost my shit laughing.

Antonio raises his eyebrows at me, and amusement shows on his face. "I'm afraid to ask, but why?"

"Wellllll," I burst into laughter just thinking about it, and take a moment to compose myself before going on. "She had a light mo, and beard"

Antonio shakes his head and starts chuckling. "What do you mean? What's so funny about that?"

"Well, that's not the funny part. All I could think about was, what if she has a partner, and when she goes down on him, does he mistake her for a dude and still get off?

"Are you serious, that's what you thought about?" I can see him trying to hold back his laughter.

I nod and try to be serious. "Yeah, that's what I thought. Would you like me to stop waxing, and you can tell me if it turns you on?"

Shaking his head, he turns to leave the room, mumbling some shit I don't catch.

"Hey, Stud" He turns back in time to catch the bottle of cream I throw at him. "I grabbed that for you."

Antonio glances at the cream in his hands, then looks back at me puzzled. "What's this for?"

"I thought you might need it, in case I give you a rash the next time I go down on you." I burst out laughing at the glare he shoots me.

"Not fucking happening," he growls before muttering something in Italian and stomping from the room.

I laugh even harder.